## Chapter C

Bodies were slumped
bitterly cold waves cr
moments as birds sang and flew throughout the sky, all was quiet all was tranquil.

Suddenly the quietness was a thing of the past noises of grumbles and movement filled the air as the bodies broke the quiet, they seemed to be waking up, their eyes dumbfounded by their location, by the looks of them and by how their mouths were gasping with what looked like shock, one could draw the conclusion they had no idea of how they had got there.

They all started rising to their feet on a large beach some nine hundred yards across with beautiful turquoise oceans that stretched as far as the eye could see out of across the horizon, the beach itself was covered in warm white sand, it had been basked in the sun for most of the day. The group were quite scared at first, some were wailing. Some were shouting, and a man amongst them turned his head getting a view of the location he was in but again perplexed about how he had even arrived at this place.

Meanwhile, another man walked over and patted him on the shoulder "Excuse me, sir, you don't happen to know how we got here" He asked.

"I'm sorry, I'm just as puzzled as you I don't know how we got here either," the guy said to the other guy while quietly scratching an itch that had appeared on the end of his nose "Well thanks anyway, what's your name by the way," the man said thanking him.

"My Name is well, uh I do not remember;" He said panicking "How do I not remember my name," the guy said nervously.

"Well, My name, ah, hold on I can't remember my name either," the other man said whilst both men were completely baffled, they both looked around with utter confusion only retaking their posture when a man shouted from the other end of the group, "How did I get here, which one of you did it" he yelled, "Which one of you abducted me?, which one of you was it?, what's my name?, why can't I remember my name? who did it?" He cried.

"At the moment none of us can remember our names, which is slightly concerning, to be honest, but we need to not worry about that now we need to focus on the right here right now, it is going to be dark soon, and who knows what is going to be out at night here," said a girl who was trying to take command.

"What do you have in mind?" said another man.

"We need to band together, we need to get some sort of shelter from the elements for the night, that forest over there, we will need firewood to keep warm during the night." said the girl with a very firm voice. The group agreed and began to move forward and walk across the beach towards the position of the forest.

They entered the forest, and it was a stark change from the beach it was dark and cold, and not a welcoming place, the group of youngish men and women wandered through the forest picking up whatever they could see around them to stand a chance of surviving what would potentially be a freezing night.

A wooden pit was dug out by hand and was filled with twigs and sticks found on the floor to build the campfire; a young man tried to start a fire by rubbing two sticks together, but it was not working it became a scramble while they still had the now dwindling sunlight, at last, a few rocks were found which were whacked together creating a spark. they pulled out dry grass and put into under the wooden piles that had been gathered they then put stones around the wood in a circular pattern, to stop it from spreading to where the campfire would be. The dried grass went up like tinder setting the wood alight and igniting the campfire.

A few guys came across big hanging grapevines, and these were quickly pulled down and handed out to the rest of the group as their first meal on the island before they tried to get some sleep.

The next day, they all awoke and decided that they were going to try and build some sort of shelter as they had come to the realisation that help could be days if not weeks away. So, the only logical thing they could do was try to survive it, they needed to band together, and a plan of action of some sort was drawn up with whatever they could get their hands on.

Everyone in the group was divided into sections, Scouting Team, and Hunting Team and Crafting team. The Scouting team was sent up the ridge to scout out food and to locate some sort of water source that could be used for drinking water,

As soon as they were ready the newly created Scouting team got straight to work, they left their makeshift camp and began to walk up the hill in the direction of the ridge, In search of food and water, they needed to find running water as soon as possible as it was a swelteringly hot day again and the hot sun was already beaming down, and dehydration was becoming a real possibility for a few. The others, however, would be focusing on building a camp for the night and the possible few nights ahead.

The scouting party walked up the ridge and across the trees to see if they could see any form of water source they searched for ages walking a mile or two and going through the trees until they came to a truly massive waterfall, flowing down into a majestic lagoon with clear water, and lush green shrubs around its edges including berries and apples and other shrubs that lead into a clearing in the forest. One man took off his shirt, found a stick, and created a bindle to hold the apples that they had found to take back to the others so that they could have some of the food found. One of the scouting team members picked what they believed to be a horn off the ground and used the hollow side to collect water from the lagoon so that could be transported back and forth.

Meanwhile, the others in the group had begun making a makeshift shelter using long wood and grass to prevent it from soaking during potential rain. Nearly everyone was chiming in as they all wanted to survive and find out why they were here on this island.

The forest track that the Scouts were following was huge and crowded with many trees down the side. Its canopy was claimed by birch, willow, and hickory, and twinkling lights bursting through their crowns allowed for a mishmash of ferns to sprout in the moss-covered grounds below. Curving creepers waved from many trees, and a variety of flowers, which were found in the quietest places, enriched the otherwise bleak and quite dull view.

An hour or two later they returned to the makeshift camp and with them they brought back apples and most importantly water which was the most important thing of all.

The rations were divided out and all were thankful for each other's commitment to maintaining each other's survival. They all slept under a grass and wood canopy that night with fires going to keep them warm but to ward off predatory animals as well.

Sunrise had dawned and there was a foul mist in the air, people were grumbling that others were stealing food and that others were hoarding supplies these theories were criticised by the group's leader at the time the girl who had suggested they find shelter on the first day of their time on the island. Although she agreed that there were not enough supplies at the time, she then proposed that the scouting team go on a mission to which she was going with them as she was on the scouting team too.

The scouting team prepared to go on an expedition and would go further out across the island and look for more food and supplies, they started to walk up towards the ridge and planned to walk up the hillside to see if they could see anything and have a look over the island.

They passed jagged rocks, and ancient trees, across the sky birds were flying, and the sound of the wind whistling against the trees until it went quiet, they had emerged into a rather big clearing.

## Chapter Two: The Fort

The clearing itself was huge, and it was right at the top of the hill looking over at the ocean from there they could see the waves crashing and the sounds of birds flying overhead "Is that what I think it is" One of the scouts said.

"Wait! Thats a Fort, well what used to be one I would expect" another exclaimed. Up ahead was an old large Run-down fort looking over toward the ocean and all one side of the island and looked the valley, in which they realised that somewhere in that forest canopy they were looking down on was their makeshift camp and where they had just come from.

The fort had been there for at least a few hundred years trees had grown into the walls but some of the now ancient walls remained strong, it had although been abandoned for a long time at least. "What do you think Happened here," someone said.

"From the looks of this place, I would say it was time itself, not everything survives the test of time you know, the great temples of old that would have looked old resplendent in there heyday but now are left to become spectators of a forgotten time, that have lasted a lifetime," said another man while they were examining an old clay pot that had been left on the floor near the door "We should check those rooms there could be old supplies leftover" someone suggested which made the other guy put down the pot he had been looking at.

That is a brilliant suggestion, this is a legitimate human settlement, there could be anything here" shouted a man as they walked into one of the few rooms that had stood the test of time in that room there was a window looking over at the bay. A barrel was in the corner which had an axe left in. They pocketed that rather quickly taking the bucket with them too with the hope of using it to collect larger quantities of water than the horn that they had been using previously. They walked around these rooms, and a girl heard a creek from under her as the floorboard suddenly gave way and she fell through the floor with it. And crashed down to earth with one terrible thud. "Are you okay down there" shouted the man who was above ground "Yes, Woah, you're going to want to see this," she said shouting up.

She had found herself in an old and forgotten room, an old stone doorway was perched in the far corner that had been long since sealed up. An old sword had been left on the floor which in turn was covered with dust and there were arrows on the floor and a few silver goblets that had been left on a wooden table that looked like it was going to cave in at any given moment.

"By the look of the dust in here, I'd say no one has stepped foot in here for at least a few centuries," she said shocked. A man put down some vines and climbed down and had a look as well "Oh my lord, this is incredible we would never have found this place if you hadn't fallen through, holy hell those planks look thick, that is quite a sizeable plank of wood, how did you snap that in half" he said.

"I don't know maybe it's because I'm on the heavier side of life and how do I know anyway, none of us can remember who we are, so I can't remember my name or who my parents are for Christ's sake," she said affirmatively.

"Sorry I didn't mean to upset you it's quite a thick plank is what I meant, and that its why I believe this has remained hidden for so long" he apologized.

"Apology accepted, but you are right I think all the earth and tree roots have weakened the planks plus the fort is quite high up so would have faced the elements over time," She said as they were rummaging around they looked at the sealed door walked over to and put their hands on the it "Whoever sealed that up didn't want anyone getting in that's for sure," he said looking around, a noise of crunching crowd the room a book was on the floor "What do we have here," She said opening it "their words in it but I don't know what language that is," she said

"Pass it to me," he said which she passed it to him, and he said, "I do not know this language either" They put the book down and found what looked to be a tunnel in the middle of the room, they started following it and it came to a massive room full of old tools. Hammers, Mallets. And nails in a round barrel lay stacked swords and old spears "This is wonderful we need to take all of this" the man shouted. In the corner, an old wagon was left gathering dust. an old chest was discovered underneath a table. They both decided to open it, much to their surprise it was filled with Seeds, which had lasted centuries and had stayed in a cold and safe environment.

Meanwhile, above ground, the other scouting members had found what looked to be an old lookout turret that still had its steps that had not eroded and could be accessed and allowed to get to the top, from the top it looked out over the sea across the desolate cliffs where birds were now resting and the noise of the sea waves crashing into the cliffs down below. The Turquoise Ocean was becoming restless which hinted that a storm was coming.

They stood on top of the turret with the wind blasting them with its cold easterly winds, one of the team then caught a glimpse of something peculiar in the corner of his eye on the cliff tops and much to their shock there was what remained of a Pirate ship clambering on the side of the cliff. "How do you suppose that got there, I mean that's got to be at least one hundred and fifty feet above sea level," someone said totally and utterly baffled.

"Maybe it was the Kraken," somebody present said jokingly.

"What's the bloody Kraken?" a girl asked shaking her head in confusion.

"A great big octopus around about a hundred feet big weighing at least five thousand pounds in weight, it with its gigantic tentacles it would have raised into the air then threw it onto the cliffs" the guy said explaining.

"Your joking" she said baffled.

"Yes, but all jokes aside possible a tsunami, maybe even just rough weather, we've only been here a day we know nothing about this island really, for all you know this island could be a volcanic hotspot, only time will tell" the man said causing a lot of the people around him to almost fall asleep "We should head over there, there may be some supplies left we could use," another scout said as they started to head down the ancient spiral steps that were small in some places CRASH a scout at the top whose foot was wider than the steps tripped and fell and he had started to roll and take out the one in front of him and a few short moments they were all together in a ball going down the stairs and landed at the bottom with one bloody great thud. "Everyone Alright," someone said.

"Yeah, you broke my fall," another said laughing they all chuckled as they all got back to their feet and started the trek to the old ship. The Others in the underground of the fort were unaware of what they had found were still searching the cavern they had discovered Farming Hoes, a few old crossbows and what must have been an old doorway, the guy noticed a pickaxe on the floor, in which they started to hack at the doorway which after a few strong swings the rocks began to fall and crumble these were moved out of the way and they took a wooden stick set fire to it and created a torch to light the way. The contents of the next room were indescribable several limitless wealth lay before their eyes. A golden table belonging to a king once probably a chair made of literal diamonds, and what shocked them most was gunpowder and old cannons that must have been at least three to four hundred years old.

The other group arrived at the Pirate ship, and it was not a pretty site, there were giant cracks and broken beams everywhere. but that is to be expected after so many years of neglect. She was hanging slightly to one side and little dents covered much of her exposed hull. A couple of chests and leftover barrels are expected remains of an interrupted journey. Bones of some sort can be seen in one of the broken ones. Fortunately were not bones of humans , because they made it out safe and unharmed hopefully at the time of whatever caused the ship to end up on the side of a cliff. She was in a roughened condition for sure; there are gaping holes all along the hull and rushed wood around its sides, and Crates, chests and barrels were left inside and held what could have been her last secrets from before her demise. The ship was in an odd, angled position and the weakest of materials had already perished to time leaving an even emptier vessel. Inside was the same bleak story and had built up vast quantities of rotting wood an old book lay on the ship floor in a small box, a guy opened the book and began to read out its contents.

*"alas Gentlemen we are defeated, our king shall look down on us with great pride, we fought thee, enemy, with great strength but at last their great fort kept us from reaching thy island, they are now pulling our ship with their wooden grabber device as our ships begin its hoist up the cliff, alas I don't have long I hear my enemies cannons being loaded aimed directly at thy head, goodbye my king Goodbye My Beloved Spain, Goodbye My Kingdom, goodbye!*

***Captain Santiago Javier Alejandro López***

*24th May 1621*

They had all gone into shock, that this book had survived in this boat for so long, the realisation that it was not a pirate ship but an old navy ship that had been here for an exceptionally long time "How long do you think that's been here."

"Well, It Arrived here on what twenty-fourth of May sixteen twenty-one but unfortunately none of us remember who we are where we are from or how we got here, we don't know the date or time, this could have been here for a few hundred or possibly thousands of years, I fear we may never know" a guy muttered as they had started to look around other parts of the old ship which they had now realised were not ruined but were intact, and inherited little more than vines due to it being taken out of the water by some contraption. upon closer examination, the ship had a few secrets still with Cannons found under the floorboards.

The others in the fort caves had found the back of the cave and had begun walking back up with the Wagon full of supplies that would come in handy for their survival. They got back up to the first room and suddenly reached the consideration of how they would get the wagon to the surface. The female took the pickaxe and started to hammer at the door breaking it piece by piece until the sealed door came crashing down. They simply rolled the wagon out of there and backed up the old spiral tunnel that would not have been used for many years. Upon reaching the surface they realised that the others had gone.

They sat down on the fort wall for what felt like an eternity until the others came back to the fort pulling a box of old treasure. "Where did you get that" the girl asked.

"We found an old, Navy warship on the cliffs, over there," another scout said pointing towards the top of the fort," the scout said.

"We need to name this fort, so we always know how where we are talking about," a guy said looking at the others and all the surrounding areas while scratching an itch on the back of his head "We should call it Cliffside Fort" someone suggested.

"Ok, all agreed Cliffside Fort it is," another man said, and they all nodded in agreement as they began the long and downward walk back towards the camp where everyone else was. The way back was challenging as they had to try and guide a wagon and chest over, brutal, and harsh terrain which they found physically and mentally exhausting, they got down to the lagoon where they found the water from the day earlier, they could physically go no further with it as they were utterly exhausted it had taken over three hours to push it the two and half miles or so they had gone from the fort. The decision was made to leave it by the lagoon and get it tomorrow. When they would have been more rested. They left it near the lagoon and made the walk down to camp where everyone else was around a mile downhill. when they arrived back there were scowls or disappointment from the others that they had come back empty-handed. "We left the stuff we found by the lagoon we couldn't take it any further we all felt exhausted with the weight and couldn't bring it down we'll go and get it down I'm sorry" one of the scouts said apologetically.

"It is ok another said, "We have all been thinking we need a leader elected, who made most of the decisions on the scouting party?" A man said.

"We all made decisions, but he was the most vocal" A girl said pointing at the guy next to her.

"Right scouting team's choice has been made and she made most of the decisions for food, he made most of the decisions for camp, he got us most of the food down here" a person said.

The Five people were put down as the perspective leaders and it was then the choice of the others who they voted for to be the chosen chief of the Colony. As they had no paper nor pens, the five candidates were blindfolded while the others placed sticks by their desired candidate and whoever had the most sticks at the end was the overall winner, to make it fair the grass was checked for no prior sticks first, that might sway the vote in favour or out of favour a candidate. This was also checked to see if a voter had more than one stick, the votes were counted, and the overall Winner was...

**Chapter Three: The Leader Is Chosen**

The Scout, His first order was to give the other colonists names, the head of Camp production was given the name Woody, The Girl in charge of food preparation was given the name Apple and the new head scout was given the name

Scoutina, and the food hunter was given the name Hunter.

These four individuals were admitted to the newly created Grand Council of the Island Colony. This was to be where the decisions would be made, and the laws would create. The island was to be governed by friendship, wisdom, and kindness to all members of the colony.

Day One of the new regime started swimmingly it was decided that if help were to come and a way off the island was going to be made a possibility they would need to be on higher ground. The idea was to relocate by the lagoon where the wagon had been left by the scouting department the day prior, and because it was higher ground and had an unobstructed view of the island and had sufficient water source. The move was not seen as smart by all the colony members but if they wanted to survive, they needed to stick together. The leader Of the Colony gave himself the name "Principal" a word for a leader or first in order. Using the old book that had been found on the navy ship's paper Woody began to draw out plans for Wooden Cabins that would be the for the colonists to live in. On the paper in bold letters, it read.

The Colony Plans

- ❏ Fifteen Houses (At the Moment)
- ❏ Thirty Males
- ❏ Thirty Females
- ❏ Office For Colony Leader
- ❏ Canteen
- ❏ Public Conveniences
- ❏ Storage Rooms

The plans were drawn out and approved by Principle, the plan for houses was for two members to share at first so there was enough for people to live in whilst more could be built. The houses were ordered to be made first and the first one was to be made immediately, using the axes retrieved from the fort, trees began to be cut and carpenters began to smooth the wood down.

A few hours later the framework of the first one was being tied and nailed together; most departments were helping the building; A wooden slopped roof was nailed down before the walls were added so they would have a place to sleep if it rained at night. The size was ten feet by fifteen feet long. Woody had them start the framework of the second house in the colony whilst others began work on another, These Houses were being built around the lagoon just up the hill from where the original camp was, this area had a running water source and viewpoint over the sea at many directions to try and locate on coming boats making it the ideal place to set up camp, it was also strategically next to the path that lead up to the fort and the navy ship behind that meaning that supplies could be brought down with ease and tree cover meant that the houses would be protected on many fronts from high winds coming in from the coast, making the area perfect for what they needed at present.

The sound of hammers hammering, Trees falling and people moving all flew around in unison, the industrialisation of the colony had well and truly begun. Principle sat on a log looking over at the colony from above looking at people carrying logs, and building timber frames, his eyes were gleaming and his mouth smiling everything was going as planned.

Woody was called to a meeting by Principle along with all the other heads of the departments. He walked into the known constructed frame but no walls meeting room where the others were sat on chopped-to-size wooden logs "Ah Woody Thank you for being able to join us, I know your schedule at the moment is busier than all of ours but still I appreciate it" Principle started.

"No problem" Woody replied taking his seat.

"Right, ladies and gents let us get down to business shall we," Principle said quietly 'What is our list of Supplies Apple" asked Principle again.

"We have around fifteen Barrels of apples, fourteen barrels of grapes, and around the same for berries," Apple said taking a sip of water from the cup that was straight in front of her was made from bamboo "We have more than enough fruit, put it that way," said apple cracking a joke.

"Good" Principle said with a smile on his face 'food is not a problem well at least not for now, this island has large quantities of it," he said happily.

"If we could get a Bucket and have people leave their seeds from their food, we could use them to grow more, we'd have an infinite supply," Apple said with a gentle smile.

"Thats a brilliant idea, do we have any free buckets at the moment," Principle said quickly.

"Not at the moment, they may be a few still at the fort that we could take," Scoutina said.

From the outside, the house looked old but wonderful. It had been built with oak wood and had mahogany wooden decorations. Tall, rounded windows let in plenty of light and had been added to the house in a very symmetric way. The roof was made of Hardened Oak wood that had been coated in tar to add strength and weather it. the houses were nearly completed they had used hardened rock and wood to build a slate-like roof that would allow the rain to slide off which in turn along with varnishing would make sure the houses would not rot and could last years if needed.

### *Chapter Four: The Unwarranted Surprise*

Hunter, head of the Hunting Department on what was thought to be day forty-five since they arrived on the island began planning a mission to look for food further on over the ridge from where the cliffside fort was located. The plan was to head out there as soon as it turned first light. The new day broke, and the hunting team began their trek up the freezing track towards the forest which would lead them up the ridge to the fort and the uncharted lands that lay behind it.

They all walked up the track picking fruit from the trees and putting them in the baskets, that they had brought with them, they grabbed apples and pears off trees. "Make sure you get as many of these as possible" Hunter Said "Actually make sure to tell the others to not throw the seeds away as I've just had an idea, we could use them to grow them down there so we can have them down there" he added.

"Okay, we have got around two barrels of pears and two barrels of apples, "A member of the team said.

"Great, Urk" Hunter Replied

"Thank you, Sir," Urk said. The names of the Hunting party had been given Urk a young male, Sula a female, Bork, another male and Barla another female, the others were Hala, Carka and Mimpa to name just a few,

Meanwhile at the camp, Woody had his team adding the finishing touches to one of the last houses, all colonists now had a house of their own.

The colony was almost finished, the farming department had begun building a farm, and fields were reaching everywhere, broken up only by gutters of water inhabited by frogs and insects.

All around you goats and sheep slept and loitered in the gentle pastures, and along the edge of the fields ran a grass-covered, dirt road which they had made themselves that led to the farm which was about a mile from the colony near where the first settlement was found on the day that they had arrived on the island itself.

The road made its way to a typical farmhouse guarded by a sleepy, old dog that they had found. The farmhouse was showing signs of wear and tear due to the farmland position in the open looking out over the bay with no protection from the forest, but in otherwise excellent condition. A tall silo was filled with silage, an outdoor kitchen including a clay oven was built to the side of the courtyard, and a small seating area provided a resting place for those enjoying some of the products sold right here on the farm. The farm had a cosy feel to it, and the beauty of the landscape only added to this. All that was needed in the colony was law and order a police officer had not been selected the position was to be called Head Marshall or Appointed Sheriff but at the time the position was vacant and ready for an occupant.

There was a plan to build a defence position in potential preparation for the need if they were attacked by animals, the island had not been explored fully, and there might have been bigger and unknown animals at other parts of the island. A nice cool breeze lingered over the island like a fly on food the hunters did not mind the temperature had been hot for the few days prior, a day of a cooler temperature would be quite nice for them. Silent tree limbs suspended from a couple of trees, and a mishmash of flowers, which were scattered sporadically, enhanced the otherwise beige lower level. a medley of noises, those of rummaging critters, echoed in the air and added to the sounds of the sound of the wind blowing gently through the forest. The leaves were starting to fall off the very tall trees, autumn was approaching fast. Bundled vines dangled from the occasional tree, and a hodgepodge of wildflowers growing here there and everywhere. Carpets of lush grasses stretched across the landscape, interrupted at times by small, wooden huts and their little gardens in the far distance back towards the colony. Tapestries of colourful blossoms stood out among the green grasses and enticed countless butterflies and crawling creatures in all shapes and sizes. High above them birds swirled and danced in the sky. A serene panorama with soft, floral scents accentuated by the warmth of a late spring's sun, occasionally veiled by delicate clouds, would be enough to calm even the most restless of souls.

The Team continued and emerged by the fort where they crossed paths with the scouting department who were at the fort grabbing some more supplies. "Looks like a good collection of tools there," Hunter said whilst popping his head into the group of people looking down at a barrel full of stuff and standing around chatting.

"Oh, Hi Hunter, where you guys off to?" Scoutina said inquisitively

"We're going to the woods that are behind the navy ship, I'm hoping we can find more variety of foods and potentially here's hoping some livestock," Hunter said with a smile.

"Anyway, enjoy the hunt" Scoutina.

"Hang on why don't your team come with us, there could be more supplies further on" Hunter suggested.

"Do you know what that is a great suggestion, yes, we do not exactly have that many supplies that we were going to take back, a few old bolt cutters and some axes that we found in an old box, but we can put them in a bag and bring them with us?" Scoutina said. Both teams walked towards the navy ship and the., the great unknown behind that. The wind was blowing, and the grass was swaying Hunter had his eyes pierced around looking through the densely packed forest, until they saw a Cow. "A Cow" Hunter shouted within seconds the hunting team sprang into action with Urk grabbing a blowpipe and aiming it towards the position of the cow "One, Two, Three" Pow! The sound of the pipe firing and the cow bolting. "Get him Again, quick before he runs" Hunter exclaimed, they fired again it missed. It took three more attempts before the cow was finally dead" Beefs on the menu tonight" Hunter shouted happily "Get this tied and up and prepared for transport.

Meanwhile, the tagging along Scouting department had opted to go down a different path and scout out a cliff ridge that had caught their eye, as they were walking along there it was a rather rocky and tough descent that saw them rise to a particularly high peak that looked over a very jagged cliff that was a sheer drop down "if you fall here, you've had it you know" said another scout

"So don't fall" Scoutina said with a bit of sarcasm as they were beginning the walk up the hill towards a flat clearing that was approaching. The temperature was rising it was around twenty-two degrees Celsius, the sun was shining, and the trees were swaying with a slightly cool breeze beginning to blow through. "We should name this the Collapsing Bluff," A member of the scouting department said. The others looked at him and laughed and he laughed too. "Thats a great name it does exactly what it says on the tin," Scoutina said laughing amidst A tumult of wild sounds, those of foraging animals, added life to the forest, and overpowered the croaks of frogs in the nearby ponds. Hunter and his team were trying to find another cow and were drawing up a plan to find a way to preserve the food for a long time. The way that they were suggesting was to bury it in a barrel of salt as salt could preserve meat.

This woodland part was limitless, bright, and flourishing. Its canopy was marked by cottonwood, cedar, and holly, and cascading lights bouncing between the leaves allowed for bright shrubs to monopolize the moss-covered grounds below. Quiet branches embraced many a tree, and a range of flowers, which grew dispersed and sparingly, brightened up the otherwise homogeneous scenery. A discord of animal noises, which were caused by insects and critters, reverberated through the air and were backed by the occasional sounds of birds of prey gliding in the air looking for their next prey, fields stretching over great distances and animals trampling through it. The noises of the hunting department running after animals could be heard through the trees.

The scouts decided to continue walking up the cliffside until one of the members stopped and looked out over the cliffside and out over the sea and the horizon beyond that "Beautifull here isn't it, you know it's picturesque" The female scout said as some singing birds flew overhead and out across horizon The sounds of animals Trampling in the distance behind some large bushes These plants grow in huge groups, but it's extremely difficult to control and maintain their growth lack of activity on the island has caused them to grow out of control and everywhere. The smell of the now beginning-to-fall leaves and the swaying grass wept up their noses, all was quiet all was nice.

Until they were spotted by a group of people looking at them around about one hundred yards further up the path "Hunter, I take it you found some animals then" Scoutina said moving lightly forward but there was no response. Scoutina started to move forward again "Move Back" someone shouted.

"I beg your pardon. Hunter," Scoutina said still moving forward.

"Move Back or Else," the guy said shouting brandishing a bow and raising it at them whilst moving forward she then realised that it was not Hunter.

"Drop the Bow," Hunter said with his men emerging out of the hedge to utter gasps of shock that then followed.

"Who are you, how did you get here" The guy shouted back lowering his bow and looking at them.

"He's not one of ours" Scoutina said turning to Hunter.

"Tell me how you got here right now!" the guy shouted with great impatience.

"We don't know," Hunter and Scoutina said in unison as they turned to look at the guy venting their frustration with this annoying guy

"I'm sorry we didn't know that there were others on the island." The man said calming down

"Others how many are you" Hunter said.

"All in all, about a hundred and ten or so what about you" the man said becoming more friendly

"There's around sixty of us" Hunter replied before putting his hand forward and saying, "My name is Hunter" They shook hands with Scoutina smiling on, a good moment for both groups, "My name is Rakansaur" he said.

"Nice to meet you Rakansaur," Hunter said looking over at him.

"Nice to meet you too" Rakansaur replied before turning to Scoutina "And what might your name be miss?"

"Scoutina" she said turning to shake his hand.

"I would like to formally apologise that we threatened you we were startled up until now we were completely unaware that there were other people other people on the island" Rakansaur said with a calm and apologetic voice.

"So, were we, up until now we had no idea your people were on the island, how long have you been here if I may ask?" Scoutina asked kindly.

"We've been here around sixty days we believe but we have not kept a record, well that being said we don't know how we got here" Rakansaur said.

"We are completely the same, we have no recollection of who we are or how we got here, but Woody our chief construction officer believes we've been here forty-fifty days or so" Hunter said calmly.

"So, you've started a camp then, we started ours a few weeks ago" Rakansaur questioned whilst looking out over the sea and into the horizon before opening his mouth "Hopefully we can all get off this island none of us knows who we are or how we got here which is freaky really." Said Rakansaur

Rakansaur was a short man around. five foot four and had quite a stubbly face covered in orange freckles and short curly hair and was quite a skinny build. Scoutina on the other hand was a large girl around five foot seven and weighed around a hundred and ninety-eight pounds. But they both were nothing to Hunter who stood at a tall six foot three and had a solid blond moustache and a chiselled jawline and had a muscular physique. They were talking about some topics, when Scoutina turned towards a member of the Hunting and scouting parties "Urk, head back and get Principle and bring him here" Scoutina said with some authority.

"Oi I'm not in your department, you can't order me about good grief" Urk retorted with a gasp of disbelief.

"Urk, do as she says and don't you ever talk back ever again!," Hunter said.

"Yes, Hunter," Urk said whilst turning and beginning the walk back to the camp. In a shocking but nice turn of events Rakansaur turned away and called out to one of his men that were standing further back "Kragon, Go tell Kanstunip that I request his presence here, he's going to want to see this" Rakansaur said whilst turning back to Hunter and Scoutina "Might as well Recognise each other" he added.

"Diplomatic talks here we come," Scoutina said laughing whilst the others all laughed as they looked out over the old and crumbling cliffs and the sea beyond. Where they noticed a dolphin jump out of the ocean as if to say hi. Down to the side of them were some little green plants., These plants grow in small groups, they plan "Those plants I have never seen anything like them" Scoutina said pointing at them.

"We called them Jungle feeds, we found that they can relieve a sore throat by being digested, we found that out as we thought they could be a potential food source" Rakansaur said looking at them "They rely on winds to carry their seeds away to reproduce. Once pollinated they grow a yellow flower with a little orange dot inside it, we discovered that when that grows that is when it becomes edible" said Rakansaur.

"That's clever, we should take seeds from here so we can grow them," Scoutina said quick thinking.

"Why did we not think about that, that's a genius idea, Bonriutus take note of that if you please, that's a genius move, it would become infinite," Rakansaur said politely.

Both messengers embarked on their respective missions to get the colony leaders and bring them to the now-named Collapsing bluff so that they could see the revelation for themselves, and whatever was to happen afterwards would be their decision and theirs alone.

## Chapter Five: Conference

Both leaders had been informed by their messengers to come to the Collapsing Bluff. "Urk please tell me why they have sent for me" Principle said quietly while walking.

"You'll see sir," Urk said.

"Look there's the fort, I haven't been up here since the day we found it, Scoutina fell through the floor, and that's how we found most of the supplies, I'm still surprised she didn't hurt herself; I mean it was a terrible thud," Principle said with a little smile as they were heading towards the navy ship and into the previously unknown regions beyond that. "Tell me did they find food" Principle asked while plodding along.

"Yes, Principle, food was found" said Urk who was trying to hurry Principle up the hill.

"Well. Why do they want me?" Principle questioned.

"The food is not why they want you, principle."

"I'm not entirely sure, I'm the one who should tell you that principle," Urk said.

"Urk, just tell me, man, for goodness's sake, please" Principle Said losing his patience.

"We were walking along the ridge and came across a whole other colony on the other side of the island" Urk said revealing the truth of why Principle was being called there.

"Another group, how long have they been here?" said Principle whose eyes lit up upon hearing this news, it interested and perked his interests "The guy said around sixty days" said Urk.

"Sixty days, so just a little more than us then?" remarked the principle.

"Yes, looks that way, sir," Urk said hurryingly.

The two men walked with a slow and easy pace, The birds flew overhead still singing their song and the trees were swaying from side to side in the midday breeze, the sounds of animals sprawling through the grass, the sound of grasshoppers buzzing and the hissing of a dragonfly's wings as they flew by. The temperature was now exceeding Thirty-five degrees Celsius. Hardly any clouds were in the sky just a few small ones scattered across the horizon.

Hunter and Scoutina had taken refuge from the sweltering heat and were sat in a shaded area under a grass canopy and covered around the sides with trees, both of their departments had been despatched to go and round up more food for the colony. While the two of them waited for Urk to return with Principle. The food that was gathered was two cows that had already been found, and a huge ton of mangos that had been growing on trees around them. A few of the scouts had found some bananas, Coconuts, Pineapples, Papaya, and watermelons, while the hunters were hunting down animals.

It was around about twenty minutes later when Urk reappeared with Principle, the two men began to walk over to Hunter and Scoutina

"Good Afternoon you two" Principle said kindly as he walked towards them.

"Hi Principle" they both said standing up to their full heights.

"Principle, the reason we have sent for you is_ --- "Scoutina was interrupted.

"I'm aware of why you both sent for me, I asked Urk, while we were walking on up, I could not understand why you called me for a food mission," Principle said.

"Okay," they both said.

"So, what are we doing now" Principle.

"At the present second, we are waiting for the gentlemen from the other colony, Rakansaur is his name to come over here and tell us that the leader has arrived" Hunter said.

"So, what do we do until then" Principle said.

"Who wants some beef," Hunter said laughing.

"Thats not funny," Scoutina said.

"I'm not joking, I'm serious who wants some beef" Hunter said impatiently. Everyone that was there began to walk around and collect parts of wood and stone to create a campfire. The stones were placed in a circle on the ground, this was to allow the fire not to spread from its designated area. They started by grabbing small bits of wood which would become the bottom layer of the fire. Scoutina had gathered dry brown grass that was sprinkled on the wood in various places this was to be used as tinder which would be used as flammable material, this could start the fire. Hunter produced an ingenious way of lighting the fire as with them they had no way of being able to light it, grabbing two fragments of flintstone Hunter bashed them together and formed a spark, the spark landed on the sprinkled grass and then at last fire.

Now that the fire had been started bigger wood could systematically begin being added to the campfire to preserve the fire and keep feeding it to get it to the right temperature to be able to cook anything. Urk however was given the slightly grim job of preparing the cow. He began to strip parts of meat off the dead cow; these strippings were given to Hunter who put them on rocks over the fire where they would be cooked.

They were on the fire for about twenty-five minutes until they were ready to eat everyone there had a piece including Principle, the sound of chomping and swallowing filled the air broken by the sound of a voice "That was delicious, that was well cooked Hunter, you'd give Apple a run for her money" Principle said approvingly.

"It was very good Hunter," Scoutina said whilst catching a glimpse in the corner of her eye of someone approaching, she blinked, and the face became clearer it was Rakansaur returning.

Rakansaur waited for a moment, then approached "Principle this is the Guy, we were telling you about, Rakansaur" Hunter said introducing them as Principle suddenly walked forward and began to shake his hand "Good day Rakansaur, my name is Principle, I'm the leader of the group behind me" Principle said in a welcoming gesture.

"Good to meet you, Mr principle my leader Kanstunip will meet you now," Rakansaur said politely.

"Thank you, and you can drop the mister, it's just principle," he said.

Rakansaur began to lead them to where his leader was located. In front of them lay a short man no taller than five foot one and with a small scraggly beard and a thick accent "You mest be Prencepel" he said with his distinct thick accent.

"While yes, and you must be Kanstunip, I take it," Principle said.

"Well, yes I em," he said while the two men were shaking hands and exchanging pleasantries and after that talks began, with both sides officially recognising each other and pledging that both colonies would never interfere with each other's rights. also included was the forest behind them on top of the collapsing bluff would be the border between the two colonies.

The two leaders got along very well and wanted to talk again about the prospects of a trade deal between them, when the talks ended both sides left feeling satisfied with what they got from the deal.

Later, Principle was walking back to camp with Hunter and Scoutina who had sent both of their colonies back down earlier on with the clear message of Do not tell anyone what you have seen up on the hill, they wanted to keep this revelation secret for now. "I want you two to know that I'm so proud of you both, this momentous day could not have been done without both of your quick thinking," Principle said with a great big smile on his big round face.

Later that night Principle met with Hunter, and Scoutina in a meeting that also included Urk, The four of them were sat around a big table with Principle at the head of the table and the other three sat around the other ends of the table "In light of what's happened today the usual logic would be to hide this information until its complete, but In this case telling the truth may just be the better option, in case they find each other and cause an absolute ruckus" Scoutina stressed

"Urk, what's your opinion?" Principle asked.

"I believe, what I see, but In this case, I agree with Scoutina," Urk said while Scoutina smiled at him "But if we don't tell them and one of ours gets startled by one of them accidentally or inadvertently does something, this could lead us to quite a precarious situation that could be avoided by telling the truth and not keeping them in the dark," Urk said

"Spoken like a true politician, thank you Urk, Hunter I might poach this one from you, and make him my assistant" Principle said proudly "We will tell them first light tomorrow, that's my decision," Principle said standing up.

The hunting department brought back the two cows well one was missing a leg which they had eaten hours previously, the debate was on how to preserve the animals. They sorted this by getting Woody to build a big wooden box filling it with salt and burying the cows in the salt to preserve the food.

The next day started early, everyone was gathered in the same place, Principle stood on a wooden stage with Hunter and Scoutina sitting on the Left of him and Urk on the right now appointed deputy leader of the Colony by Principle "Good Morning everyone, yesterday I was made aware of a shocking discovery, our scouts and our hunting departments came across people from another colony at the other side of the island, I was informed and went to meet with their leader, who we have done a deal that sticks a border on top of the collapsing bluff, that runs across the cliff. The possibility of a trade deal is being discussed as we speak" Principle told them, surprised that there were no sudden gasps of shock, and they took it in like it was nothing.

The Revelation did not affect anything that day, Woody, and his team finished the Canteen building that they were working on their next phase of the plan was to start building furniture to furnish, Tables, chairs and shelves had all been built, and they had been nailed together then sanded down, then varnished to weather it so it would not rot, these were then added into the colonists houses. Deputy leader Urk walked into the wooden house that was currently being fitted looking for Woody. He looked around and asked a gentleman who walked in with some furniture "Where's Woody."

"He was here, five minutes ago, he's gone to check on Neil the Nail maker he accidentally hammered a nail into his finger," the gentlemen said.

"Okay, which way did he go," Urk asked.

"He went left, should be the next row of houses, four houses down, that's Neil's that's where he is" the gentlemen said again.

"Thank you, what's your name by the way" Urk asked nicely.

"My name's Hurdip Sir" Hurdip said whilst placing the small table he had been handed by the other guy who had walked in and past to him whilst they were talking. Urk walked out of the door and went in the direction he was told Woody had gone. But he did not have to walk far as Woody came around the corner and caught Urk by surprise Urk let out a scream "Woody you caught me by Surprise" Urk said whilst breathing heavily.

"Sorry about that Urk, anyway is there a reason you're here," Woody told him unapologetically.

"Yes, can you begin to plan out a warehouse for food storage, Principle's orders, and Hunter's team found Cows, yesterday as you know, they have found more and need a place to store them," Urk asked.

"I'll send My men and have them build something; it could be around 25 feet that's my prediction" Woody calculated.

"Great, Principle will be pleased, anyway I will give him the news and you can get on with whatever, you are doing.

"See you later Urk, actually wait, congratulations on your promotion" Woody said proudly.

"Ah, thanks mate, feels a bit weird no longer being in the hunting department and not being in any department really," Urk said "but it's a new challenge and a fun one at that." Meanwhile, the scouts had come across a big cave just past the navy ship, left of the path that led to the collapsing bluff, "Scoutina should we go in it or leave it" a scout said.

"I would say go in, as it's looking big, and looking at those fragments it looks manmade," Scoutina said using her intuition that the plan was made, and they grabbed a few lights and walked into the cave. the temperature was a lot cooler in there it was around ten degrees lower, they walked further in and were hit by a stunning discovery "It's a gold mine" Scoutina said excitedly.

"Wait till the others find this out, there is so much of it, there's enough for everyone," someone said.

"Let's not think about greed, thank you Heup" Scoutina said butting the man in his place and bringing him back to his senses.

"No, we can use this for lots of stuff, which looks like silver and ruby to me, this is an ore mine, it might have sapphire and diamonds further down," Heup said. Suddenly out of the darkness came a rail and an old waggon that would have been used to wheel the mined ores up from deeper down the mine.

Scoutina split her department into four groups of three and sent them to separate locations in the mine to scout out parts of the mine to explore a greater range of the mine. The Mines were huge going deep into the earth and having massive quantities of Gold, sapphire, and stone, the deeper they went the mine just kept going and going, huge quantities of coal were also in the ground here, which they knew could use in fireplaces as a fuel source for fire in the upcoming winter months. Scoutina and two other scouts Ugona and Bordan were looking further down at the mine and that is where they came across fragments of platinum, one of the rarest and most expensive ores in the world. The sheer amount of it that they had found was impressive on its own. The caves were vast, but its roof was getting lower and lower the further they went in, to the point where the tall Scoutina around Five-foot- seven's head was just skimming past the roof of the cave anyone taller than five-foot-seven would not fit in this part of the cave. Which was why the six-foot-four Bordan had decided to not go further over fears he would get stuck. The other groups of the scouting department were all having the same dilemma the heights of some of the members were an issue for them in the smaller parts of the mine.

Further down the tunnel, they came to a sudden stop there were two possible ways to go left and right, Scoutina went right and Ugona went left, these tunnels were getting narrower until Scoutina who was of a large build turned back as she realized that if she went much further there was a real chance, she would not physically fit through the gap that would be there. Elsewhere Ugona was having the same issue but had reached the end of the tunnel and had decided to turn back the way she had come. She met Scoutina back at the turning point "Did you find anything" Scoutina Asked

"Just a back wall, What about You?" Ugona asked

"The tunnel leads on but was getting narrower, due to how my size, well my height wasn't the issue, due to how big that I am around the waist area I couldn't fit through "Scoutina said

"Do you want me to go and have a look and see if I can find anything there, Afterall I'm shorter and skinnier it shouldn't be a problem for me?" Ugona asked

"Well, you can try, but if it gets too narrow come back, as I will not physically be able to get there if you do get stuck," Scoutina said with caution

"Okay, Scoutina," Ugona said quietly as she began to walk into the other tunnel that Scoutina had been in previously, upon getting to the part where it got a bit too narrow for Scoutina Ugona passed through without a hitch and went down the tunnel which surprising went wider as you passed that one bit, the tunnel then opened up to a massive cave opening that had a pool in the middle with Crystal clear water. above there was a gaping great hole that looked up into the sky, it was an opening into the cave, large vines sprawled down through it, and a huge waterfall dropped elegantly down from it, Ugona put her hand into the water to her great surprise it was warm it was a hot spring. Ugona without instinct began removing her clothes and went for a quick swim, the swimming in a way was therapeutic relaxing every bone in her body and physically putting her at ease, after about twenty-five minutes she realized that she'd be gone for over thirty minutes and Scoutina would believe that she had got stuck, she hurriedly put her clothes back on and began to make her way back down the tunnel, she went around the bend and walked down the widening tunnel finding Scoutina where she had left her "I was beginning to think you'd got stuck" Scoutina said jokingly

"Sorry about that, where you found it was becoming narrower, it gets narrower then gets wider again, it goes into a massive cave opening where there's a massive hole in the cliff with vines shooting down, and there's a pool of water there quite a deep pool of water, clear water, it's also a hot spring," Ugona told her

"You swam in there didn't you," Scoutina asked

"Guilty as Charged," Ugona said

"How narrow is it height-wise there" Scoutina asked whilst looking down at the now dark tunnel

"Well, the bend where you couldn't continue is tall enough, but the narrowness is the issue, the only other issue is the area where Bordan is to do the height of the tunnel" Ugona remarked

"So, if we were to make those two parts wider and taller, we could all use that on our days off" Scoutina questioned

"Yeah, if we do make those bigger then yeah, we could all use it" Ugona said as they both began to walk back to where Bordan was waiting for them, the three of them walked back into the main part of the mine itself and found another side tunnel to explore. These mines are endless, there is so much stuff, there must be a lifetime of resources here, that we can use we have hit the honeycomb in many ways" Bordan said

"We have hit something all right this incredible what we have found has lots of value we found wealth in a way," Scoutina said smiling whilst turning the torch towards a dark area in the back wall, which was then discovered to not be the back wall at all but led to another winding cave opening that this time was a lot higher meaning that they could all past down it with no issues. The tunnel was long and straight leading to a vast old room with what looked to be like some old furnaces "This where taken the ores and melted them down, I'd expect that over there would have been the moulds" Bordan said whilst walking over "Ah yes, you see, sword, axe, these would have been the Molds for them, Iron most probably would have been here and poured in and this part would have surrounded by the hilt and thus making a sword" Bordan explained

Meanwhile, another of the split groups of the scouting department had stumbled across an office-like room closer to the mine entrance it was fairly dusty and looked like it had been untouched for many years, this room had what remained of an old table and on that table, there was old dusty candlelight that had long since burned out, an old ink pot that still had the remnants of an old quill still left in the pot, a draw was built into the bottom of the table which include an old book well, an old journal more likely The Title read *The Great Survey;*

*Date 11th August 1777*

*After being Governor for the last eighteen years that is it, I will be the last, after holding this island for over 250 years we have been given the order to retreat from the island, due to its location in the middle of literal nowhere a thousand miles probably from the nearest settlement, I have full confidence that no one will ever read this letter nor step foot on this island, why must the empire relinquish this magnificent island, that I will never understand, why must we go to fight wars started by others, The last mining figures are in*

| *Ore Type* | *Amount Mined* |
|---|---|
| *Gold* | *300,000 Barrels* |
| *Diamond* | *100 Barrels* |

| Ruby | 11,0000 Barrels |
| --- | --- |
| Emerald | 300 Barrels |
| Platinum | 7 Barrels |
| Iron | 970,000 Barrels |
| Copper | 1,300,000 Barrels |

*These Are the Final Mined Units collected over our time since our discovery of the island on April 19$^{th}$, 1527.*

*Signed – Captain Thomas Charles Henry – Governor of the Island April 19$^{th}$, 1759 – August 11$^{th}$, 1777.*

The Context of the book was a detailed Diary by the island's last governor and documented everything they had ever mined on the island in their two hundred and fifty-year ownership of the island, the documents had been signed and had been left in an old cupboard for a very long time.

The book entry was read aloud to gasps of shock, "this was written over 150 years after the navy ship incident document whoever wrote this was on the other side" a guy said.

"Well, he wasn't most of those soldiers stationed here would have been between 18 and 35 so if he was there then he'd be between 174 and 191 if he was there no, he was not he was on the same side of them but not alive as he would be unhuman if he lived that long," another said.

"Sometimes I say before I think," the guy said.

"Never mind Frup, it happens to us all," The other said.

"Thanks, Grun" Frup said kindly as they put the book back in the draw and left it like it was never touched, in a way the book was right no one would read it again only they knew the book was in there and they had read the contents and most probably wouldn't have needed to read it again.

The Mines were still ever-expanding, and the groups were finding endless caverns leading in many directions, on each side were huge quantities of gold, more gold than you could imagine. Up in front there was a black spot drawing ever nearer, upon putting a wooden torch on it, it was a sealed doorway that had been sealed with mortar made from clay that was used to seal all the cracks making it look as if there was no doorway there at all. Scoutina made the call for bordan to go back to the main entrance and get a pickaxe, so they could open the sealed doorway and find the mystery of it while it was sealed in the first place.

The other groups who had all regrouped found Bordan who had now got back, and they all joined him in going back to the sealed doorway to unlock the secrets of the sealed door, they walked through the many chasms until they reached the door "Right you lot did you find anything" Scoutina said.

"An old book entry that was from the last governor of the island they left the island unexpectedly in August 1777 the book shared what had been mined from here in the 250 years that they had been on the island," Grun said whilst looking at Scoutina.

"How much was mined from here" Scoutina asked.

"Documents said hundreds of thousands of barrels" Grun replied as bordan was standing ready with the pickaxe.

"Should I begin?" Bordan asked.

"Yes, everyone please stand well clear" Scoutina ordered as bordan began to swing aimlessly at the door it took him many swipes even taking a break due to the gruelling pain that he had received from the constant swinging he hardly made a dent into the doorway and only made a small incision into the top, as his break had ended he picked it up again and went back to it, it took hundreds of swings until the hole was big enough to climb through. The Scouts began climbing into the dark room that was now lit up as they looked around. The room was filled with swords, they looked new, sealed doors and the sheer fact that it was in a cave meant that air could not get in meant that they could not rust or gather dust, they were lying in wait for someone to find them. Further back there were shields and bows and arrows, crossbows, and one beautiful sword encrusted with diamonds laid into the handle it would no doubt have belonged to someone with a high ranking, on the roof there was a painting of a man a powerful man that of a king, a rather large king. Across the wall there was a door leading to some steps down, they followed these steps down which spiraled and spiraled until they came to a beach, as they looked up, they realized where they were they were below the Collapsing bluff on the beach which they could not see do to the overhanging ridge of the cliffs. The beach was a small cove "I'd expect this is where supplies were brought by passing vessels, the sea was probably against the cliffs in them days" Scoutina said intelligently.

"The sea looks like it's gone back in years, but as well we don't remember how we got here or who we were before the island, so we don't know what year it is really, that could have been over a thousand years ago" Ugona replied the call was made to head back up the staircase, but Ugona noticed a doorway behind them with a wooden door that was intact surprisingly pulling the handle down hard the door came off the hinges in a terrible fud. Behind this door laid one thing the farming department would be so happy with seeds. These were in a massive bag labelled potatoes, wheat, carrots, and beetroots "Apple will be happy with these take the bags, and go give them to Apple, Bordan, Grun, and Ugona remain here, the rest of you take those back and get them to Apple, quickly fast as you can" Scoutina said with some real authority.

Those not allowed to stay left with the heavy bags; they took them back up the stairs, then took the wagons from the mine and began to wheel them back to camp, it took all of them to push them over some of the harsh terrain. The move to the fort was particularly challenging and brutal to the point where Hagan one of the scouts was told to run down the path and get help. Hagan darted off at a lightning-quick pace, he began to run at a steady pace, it took him around ten minutes to reach the camp and he went to find Urk who was sitting with Principle "Urk Can you, please send us some help" Hagan asked.

"What is it, you want" Urk Said

"Scoutina, sent us back with bags of seeds, that we found in an abandoned mine, using old wagons we found we're bringing them down, but we need a few more people as we're having trouble getting it down through the terrain behind the navy ship," Hagan asked.

"What type of seeds, Hagan?" Principle piped up.

"Wheat, Carrots, Beetroots and stuff like that" Hagan answered.

"Urk, gather as many men as you can get to go help" Principle ordered.

"Yes, Principle, Hagan you better come with me" Urk said as the two of them walked out of the room to go and round up as many men as they physically get their hands on. Soon enough they had around twenty men ready to go and help them get the seeds down. The walk-up took them around about twenty minutes to do, and they arrived at the scouts trying everything to pull the wagon over the little hill. The arrival of the helping hands was deeply needed, and they simply combined strength and lifted the wagon over the little hill walked forward towards the flatter grass and placed it down, they then went back and did it for the other six wagons that they had been dragging back. The walk down now was far much simpler as it was smoother as it had been traversed hundreds of times by the Hunters, the Scouts and by others just on a walk the constant movement had kept the paths flat this in turn made it easier for them to get the wagons down.

After twenty minutes they were down and were taken to Apple who had them put in the storage room that Woody had just finished where the seeds could be kept and stored for as long as possible not be allowed to rot, which would give them a nearly endless supply of crops that could be sown. "This is outstanding where did you get all this from," Apple said.

"Our scouts found them in an abandoned mine," Urk said.

"Bloody hell, I love Scoutina, she's a diamond for bringing these down, she a scout, she didn't have to send her team down to bring us these," Apple said with a full appraisal of Scoutina.

"She cares about the Colony itself, not just the people under her" Urk said kindly as walked away and back to the meeting he was having with Principle.

Back at the Mine Scoutina, Ugona, Bordan and Grun had continued looking around and were set to leave and walked up the hill and had come back to where the path leads to the Collapsing Bluff when they heard a faint voice "Well, Then what do we have here" they turned to see a man and a few others standing there looking at them "Are you lost?" the guy said sarcastically

"Are you, you're not meant to be here, the border is back over there?" Scoutina said cockily but not mockingly.

"Oi, Girl, do I look like a care where the border is this is our land, all of it, you don't belong here, this island is ours and ours alone, do you get it, now get lost" the guy shouted.

"Your leader Kanstunip has done a deal with us you stick to your side of the border, and we'll stick to ours" Scoutina reasoned.

"Good Grief a bitch speaking to me like that, as if she has a real role in the world, Come on Return to camp, we'll deal with these invaders some other day," The guy said as his men turned towards the collapsing bluff and walked away. The scouts got ready to walk back, But Ugona looked at Scoutina who was white as a sheep shaking uncontrollably and looking as if she was about to have a few tears burst down her face "Scoutina are you alright?" Ugona asked her warmly grabbing her shoulder which scoutina turned and looked at her

"Seriously Ugona I'm fine, It's just that it's just that I have never have I been spoken to like that I did not expect that," Scoutina said quietly still shaking in shock "Come on we will go and tell Principle, about what's happened, that's a plain violation of the deal they have agreed upon," Ugona said firmly.

"Yes, also good job, you're my new Deputy Congratulations" Scoutina said smiling whilst shaking her hand, standing up to her full height, and beginning the long walk back to camp. Unbeknownst to the scouts, the hunting team had also had a run-in with some other colonists who were far from friendly that day and were adamant that the rich diverse areas that were close to the mines were their lands and they were beyond furious that they were not on their side of the border.

Many hours later Principle sat down behind his desk that had the ink and quill of an old book that he had commandeered from the navy ship, the door flung open and in came Ugona helping a shaken Scoutina upon seeing this principle stood up and walked towards them "My dear Scoutina, what an ever is the matter?" he asked wholeheartedly.

"She's a bit shaken, we had a run-in with a group from the other colony they were on our side of the border and the leader was quite rude and misogynistic, believed that this island was theirs and there's alone, they went but his last word to them while on our land was that they'd deal with us invaders another day," Ugona told Principle.

"Scoutina, you're on break for a few days, Ugona your acting head scout for the time being," Principle said with great care. "Ugona, can you leave us" Principle said again

"Of course, principle," She said as she walked out of the room leaving Principle with the shaken Scoutina he looked at her and she looked at him then he spoke "Forget about what they said, you know who you are, your scoutina, everything out there is because of you, you found the supplies, you found the mines and the seeds, you've done more than anyone could've asked for, our survival is because of you, on that beach on day one you organized everyone, stand tall, stand proud, and never give up, and never give in, braveheart Scoutina braveheart" Principle said this made Scoutina smile "Thanks Principle" cried Scoutina as stood up to leave but was stopped in her tracks as principle grabbed her and gave her a cuddle which her face mellowed and she gave somewhat of a smile.

A few hours later Hunter went and told Principle the same story about the group from the other colony getting aggressive over the food in the area and demanding the land, principle brought up scoutina and the scouts ran in with the other colonists and the same story was being repeated crossing the border.

The next day Principle met with Rakansaur from the other colony and told him what had happened, he full-heartedly apologized "I can only apologise I will talk to Kanstunip about this, this will not be tolerated and I will personally see to it myself that this will be resulted immediately, Scoutina when I met her was nothing but kind and sweet to me, for her to be treated like that is beyond shameful, whoever has done it will punished for sure, I can't stress enough how deeply sorry I am," Rakansaur said with a great sorrow in his eyes

"Thank you, Rakansaur" Principle said as both men parted ways, Rakansaur began to walk back to his camp he went back across the collapsing bluff down past some long dangling vines and walked down the other side of the cliffs he walked down a flat path which went by an old stone outpost and a few some old yurts that they had found and built up. The walk down had taken him around fifty minutes since he had spoken to Principle, he walked through their encampment and went to Kanstunip's tent "Sir can I come in" Rakansaur said.

"Who is it?" Kanstunip shouted with his thick accent.

"It's Rakansaur Sir," he said politely.

"Very well come in Rakansaur" Kanstunip said kindly as the zip of the tent moved up and Rakansaur stepped in and sat down "What do you want?" Kanstunip asked him.

"I spoke with the principle of the other colony, he said to me some of our groups waltzed over the border yesterday deep into their territory and became aggressive with their hunting department they claimed should not be allowed to forage for food there, and they head of the Scouting department her names Scoutina you met her in the conference a very kind and sweet girl was verbally abused and inundated with misogynistic comments," Rakansaur said

"We need to find out who did that, that is not acceptable, we have females in this colony who cannot be subjected to stuff like that, this will be looked at in thorough investigation, it has to be, in fact, Rakansaur you're going to look into it," Kanstunip said.

"Okay, sir, I will begin to look into it, who went out yesterday" Rakansaur asked.

"Hunting and Farming" Kanstunip said as Rakansaur stood up and walked out, his mission was to track down both departments to find out what happened. He walked down to their tent ready to look for their leader "Gurn can you give me five minutes of your time" He asked.

"Yes, what do you need" Gurn asked.

"Who did you send out yesterday" He questioned.

"Hap, Gurlic, Orn and Mintin, why do you ask," Gurn asked quietly.

"The other colony who are on the other side of the island, apparently two of our departments walked into their territory and in one case their scouting department leader was met with vile misogynistic comments, Kanstunip wants to find out who did it and fast," Rakansaur said.

"It would have been Orn, he came back yesterday and was babbling on about some whore who had stepped above her paygrade and was mouthy and bang out of order and was in our territory, I will send him to Kanstunip straight away should I tell him why he's going?," he said very much ashamed of his subordinate "No, if he knows he will plan his answers if we want to catch him out we must get him on the spot, we need to sort this out double quick," said Rakansaur

The rest of the day went fast Orn was publicly humiliated by Kanstunip for violating the agreement set in place about the borders on the island and was humiliated again for his misogynistic remarks. "We have a deal in place please do not violate this agreement as the prospects of a trade deal between us could benefit us in the long run," Kanstunip told his people as they sat and had dinner a soup made from Tomatoes, Onions and herbs, there was grumbling that night, the food issue had started to cause issues, people were starting to fall out with Kanstunip, his support was rapidly dwindling and his leadership on an edge of a knife.

## *Chapter Six: The Revenge of The Disillusioned*

Rakansaur's Investigation the day prior did not have him in the good books of the other colonists, but he was not blamed, it was Kanstunip they were blaming, they blamed him for signing a deal with invaders, with people who had all the best areas for food. Kanstunip pulled together a meeting to discuss the dismay. Rakansaur entered the room and sat down. There were six people in that room sitting around a circular table. "Dismay is on the rise, they are mad because of our struggles of getting food, and their anger has doubled since we discovered the others on the other side of the island, we must find a way to ease the situation, or more tension will arise, we need to find food of some sort, any suggestions" Kanstunip urged

"We need seeds, but people are getting angrier by the day," a guy said.

"Yes, at the moment I'm hearing that people are starting to want me replaced as leader, we need to get them back on the side or we are going to get into a lot more trouble" Kanstunip retorted the mood in the room was one of unease, all that could go wrong was going wrong. Rakansaur could see that the council was in disarray, "Could we not simply in a deal ask for seeds, in exchange for us giving them maybe two of our chickens" Rakansaur asked.

"Thats the most reasonable thing any of you have said in the last half hour, thanks Raks, that is a possibility that we could look into, actually Rakansaur you have been a good representative for us, speak to their leadership see if you can get deal for some seeds then by all means try" said Kanstunip  The meeting was ended and Rakansaur sent a messenger to newly appointed the deputy leader of the colony Urk, asking for a meeting with principle.  That day went quickly, people were still moaning the messenger came back with a handwritten letter from Urk which read.

*Dear Rakansaur*

*Thank you for the messenger, I have spoken with Principle, and he is willing to meet with you on top of the collapsing bluff at midday tomorrow, if there is anything you require, please send us a letter, and have your messenger bring it to us,*

*Kind Regards Urk – Deputy Leader of the Eastern Colony*

Grumbling went on throughout the day, Kanstunip chaired another meeting later in the day with support dropping the same people sat around the table again "Food Supplies are dropping, we don't have enough to feed everyone" said Kanstunip who looked like a man who had run out of ideas.

"Kanstunip, I have arranged a meeting with Principal Tomorrow at Midday, I will take the chickens and arrange a deal for some seeds," Said Rakansaur the only person in the room not with his head in his hands

"Good, we need those seeds, now more than ever" Kanstunip said regaining some composure 'without those seeds, we are as good as dead, we need farming to farm like the wind, Frin get your department to prepare a patch to sow as soon as possible" Rakansaur ordered.

The meeting had long since ended some of the colony's members were muttering "It's his fault you know"

"Who" someone said as they were all sat around the campfire "Kanstunip, he's weak, he should have told that other colony to leave the island, they have it all you know, from what I hear wooden houses, food, if it wasn't for Kanstunip we'd have food, he wants it all for himself" another guy said with great anger while they sat around a small fire and toasted whatever they could get their hands on, it was a rather cold night with a tinge of ice in the air. The unease was ripe that night grumbling was heard everywhere.

Meanwhile at the other Camp Principle had given the chicken to Apple who had decided to breed them not eat them, this would allow for a more infinite food supply.


The next day was more of the same Support was dropping each day, Rakansaur had started the day early in preparation for his only chance of a trade deal with Principle at midday, he was their last hope so much so Kanstunip personally met with him in the morning and wished him luck, he started to walk to the collapsing bluff around an hour and half before, he Had with him a table and a table cloth that had been made by his colony, he planned to use it as a table for diplomatic talks, he also brought with him two table chairs. As soon as Midday struck the table was set and he was their Principle and Urk both turned up at bang on midday "Principle How are You" Rakansaur said

"I'm Good, how about You" Principle replied as he was taking his seat

"I'm good, first off your word with me the other day, we held an investigation into the verbal abuse of scoutina, our colonist who was to blame has been punished, and has been suspended, please accept our full apologies no one should go through that" Rakansaur said kindly

"At least that's been dealt with, is that why you have called us" Principle Said

"Yes and no, we would like to offer these two chickens "He pulled a box with two chickens on the table "In Exchange for a bag of seeds, we are struggling now, you are our last hope, and we need your help," Rakansaur said

"It's A deal, not because of them, because of you, you investigated your colony to help find who abused our beloved Scoutina, this is the best we can do, I will have Hunter drop by later with the seeds for you," Principle said smiling

"Thank you, I am forever grateful," said Rakansaur as he passed the box of the chickens to Principle which he took and stood up 'Goodluck Rakansaur' Principle said whilst leaving

"Thank You Principle," he said as he packed up the foldaway table that he had brought with him and called for his assistant who was waiting nearby to grab the chairs. The day had gone swimmingly, the proposed trade deal had been signed, and one thing had finally gone right for

Kanstunip. The noise around the camp was one of happiness but unease remained Rumors had begun to spread about how the seeds had been gathered "A trade deal, should have just killed this Principle and forcefully taken it, everything of theirs is ours as they don't belong here, giving our chickens for them good grief, these invaders have Kanstunip in their pocket" A guy grumbled while the person next to him said "at least we got food, he brought us this far"

"We should just feel happy that we have got the seeds," the guy said as they sat around the warm campfire and were toasting little bits of chicken.

Meanwhile, Hunter and his team arrived at the other camp and handed over the seeds to their food department Kanstunip went over to say hello and truly thank them for their kindness. He then asked them "Please give my many thanks to Principle"

Rakansaur was now on the good books of his compatriots again for his negotiation skill and his exploits in getting this deal had landed him the thanks of many of the others, the food problem was over. Hunter and his team left and started to walk back to their encampment, they spotted pigs across their border, and they sprang into action maneuvering into key positions to capture and get the pigs. The Order was given not to kill the pig sending a messenger down ahead to get Woody to quickly make a Wooden fence to keep the two pigs in hoping to breed the pigs so they would have a nearly endless supply of meat, improving and balancing the diets of the colonists themselves. The sound of running in different directions as they made noises to lure the pigs down into the capture area, the first pig was easy to catch, but the male pig managed to slip away and it took many huntsmen to even attempt catching him, as the pig was so quick, until they finally caught it, they had been there for over an hour by then.

When they arrived back at camp, Woody and his craftsmen had made a makeshift pen by using leftover chopped wood that was left in storage, it was left in case there were any hiccups when they were building the houses initially, the pen was made to last and was built down on the farm. The Pigs were given to the farmers, who had begun planning where the seeds were going to be used next spring if they were not rescued off the island before then.

Over the next few days, a violent storm came through intense winds whipped the islands, leaves blew across the floor, trees fell, and in the colony, tools were flying across the ground, they buildings, however, remained strong, and the incredible craftsmanship of Woody and his team had truly been realized, Meanwhile the other colony were not so fortunate, tents had blown away during the night, buckets full of items had blown away, some people were close to hyperthermia. Everything was going wrong; meetings had been convened throughout with nothing being decided. The people had had enough. "Kanstunip has brought us to ruin, food has been destroyed, our homes destroyed, his inaction had made us a laughingstock, the other islanders will look at us with giggles, with laughter, so who do we blame?" a guy shouted standing above hosts of other people

"Kanstunip" They shouted

"Who?" He said again

"Kanstunip" they shouted again

"So, what do we say? what do we say?" He roared

"Resign, Step Down" They roared back

"Resign, no, Step down, no, Tonight we burn down his tent and remove him by force, a new leader is needed, a leader who listens to what the people want and when they want it and we want it now, Kanstunip has failed us, he has forsaken us, we remove him and we remove him now, " He roared the day was met with shock and horror rage reigned high. Rakansaur knew that by the day's end change was coming his only redeeming quality was that his negotiations saved him from shame by the others.

The sound never ending drums pierced through the frosty night sky, and the sound of anger, and rage ran wild a sudden, violent coup was unfolding In front of their eyes the council building had stone bricks go through it followed by a flamed wooden javelin which was set the table on fire, and quickly evolved to engulf the whole building, this left a torrid heat that was so hot one gentleman decided to toast a chicken next to it, Boxes were thrown aside, tools dumped across the floor, the revolution had well and truly begun Kanstunip was Physically dragged from his tent naked and thrown in a field of wet mud to add more insult to injury, they then locked him in a wooden box with a few eye holes and a hole for food to be passed through. "You want my leadership, you can have it, look what you caused, the fires, are spreading the seed is set, you have caused all of this, why cause this Grawl?" Kanstunip said angrily

"What I am causing, don't you see?" He shouted pointing at him, 'You are the reason this is happening" Grawl laughed mocking him

"I caused nothing, you are nothing but an arrogant man, who seeks power above all else, who seeks validation but offers none in return," Kanstunip said shouting back

"I'm neither, I am salvation, I am the future," Grawl said smugly

"What is it exactly, you want from all of this?" he flared back

"Control, I'm Colony leader now, your inaction has cost the lives of ten colonists, do you have no shame?" Grawl boomed taking control of the colony and everyone in it, the fire was raging the tents of the councils were alight and there was nothing to stop it, Rakansaur had escaped with his tent not burnt and was not convicted of anything, Grawl was announced as Leader standing on a plinth in front of the colony, with Kanstunip's wooden cell directly behind, Grawl looked across them happy, smiling and he began to Speak "There will be a day, where we make our society, our farms, our weapons, we will build our villages, our forts, and build our navy, our army, And that day is upon us now, The deals with the other colonists are now null and void, any rules agreed cancelled, For the Colony for the People" an amplitude of noise erupted as Grawl took over. The change was almost immediate, there was a different feel in the air, and a wave of new optimism and hope filled the encampment. Kanstunip stood in his cell and had eyes rimmed with tears. Everything they had built was about to be weaponized and industrialized.

The next day a new council was formed and no one who had been a part of the last one was invited to be in attendance, not even Rakansaur had been invited and at present he was one of the only members who had been spared criticism. The decision of what do to with the traitorous Kanstunip was up for debate, but in essence, was less of a debate and more of a kangaroo court with the pre-determined narrative already been picked, so it was no surprise to anyone when the news filtered through that News that day that Kanstunip was due to be executed the following day at midday.

Rakansaur sat in his tent utterly shocked he could hardly believe his eyes at what had happened over the last few hours. To the point he decided to go and say his goodbyes to Kanstunip, he walked out of his tent it was dark and there was no one around, he crept up to Kanstunip's Cell "Kanstunip" he called

"Rakansaur, what do you want?" Kanstunip said

"I thought, I'd come and say my goodbyes, it's not right you know, they can't do this, they have no right," said Rakansaur firmly

"What'll be will be, Rakansaur, but right now, you need to keep your head down if Grawl has any idea, you spoke to me or spoke against him, you'll be like me in here, and facing a kangaroo court as I have, and I don't want that for you!, you are better than I ever was, you'd be a much better leader than I was," said Kanstunip sympathetically

"You're still better, you're always going to be my leader Kanstunip, not Grawl, you're my leader," Rakansaur said

"My dear Rakansaur, thank you for everything, look out for yourself, my friend," Said Kanstunip kindly

The day of the execution dawned; he was to be Hung at Midday. The day was one of tension and jubilation the hanging was going to be a sight to be held, a traitor was going to have it handed to him, he was going to be shown the price of treachery, and law and order were going to be enforced and people would finally learn. Grawl's revolution had succeeded he had launched himself to universal appraisal for doing the honourable and taking out the enemy from within Kanstunip and his hack jobs.

At midday in the village centre they led Kanstunip a small man five foot one in shoes around 5ft without them was led to the makeshift gallows, he had the rope put around his neck and the most humiliating thing of all they made him wash, then paraded him naked through the village and forced him to be executed naked, they stood him on a chair but stopped and allowed Grawl to speak, "Kanstunip I will allow you speak your last words what are they?" shouted Grawl

"At least I'm going out the way I came" said Kanstunip causing everyone to laugh even Grawl let out a little giggle very few people would drop a joke before they were executed.

The chair was kicked from under him, the rope went tight, and his body swung from side to side gasping for air until his body went limp and he was dead.

Rakansaur having had to watch that grim sight sent a letter to Urk, warning him of these events knowing that Grawl would forgo all the agreements that Kanstunip and Principle had been discussing in the third conference they had a few weeks previously, which even thought of that sent shivers down his spine, knowing that a great deal of work had gone of the cliffs faster than they could achieve it.

*Dear Urk*

*I'm writing to you with the uttermost Urgency, please inform Principle, that I will likely face repercussions if my colony were to ever find this letter, Kanstunip was overthrown late last night and has been executed in the past hours, I'm writing to you to warn you the new leader Grawl, I fear will not abide by the agreements we have made, Although I hope none comes of this I pray this letter gives you the heads up of the present events in these troubling times if it was ever to come true...*

*Yours Faithfully*

*Rakansaur*

Rather than give it to a messenger who may read it, Rakansaur elected to take it up to the collapsing bluff and leave it somewhere across there, but he had realized that they could break the border agreement and find it, he, therefore, decided he would walk across the border and find them himself, it took him about an hour to reach the collapsing bluff and saw the Wooden pole placed down on what marked the border of the colonies, he passed that and walked down but he was sighted not by someone in his colony but there's "Rakansaur" Someone shouted it was Scoutina and Principle who were both out for a walk "Afternoon Principle, Afternoon Scoutina" He said politely

"What are you doing here," Principle said whilst standing with Scoutina

"Looking for you actually," he said happily

"Oh Okay, is there something you need?" questioned Principle

"Somewhere private to talk actually, I'm hoping no one from your colony or my Colony hear this" Rakansaur said hopefully

"There's a mine this way, only the Scouts know about it" Scoutina said reassuringly as all three of them walked towards the mine and down into one of the rooms in there "What is it you need to tell me about" Principle said with Scoutina closely watching

"I'm here to warn you, a revolution was launched last night and Kanstunip has been removed and was executed this morning," Rakansaur said looking around to see if anyone was listening

"Oh, my god, was it quick, please tell me it was quick" Scoutina said

"No, unfortunately, it took a while it was hanging; I feel sick watching what they did, they removed his clothes and forced him to die naked"

"They what!!!" Scoutina gasped

"They paraded him naked through the village and hung him in the centre naked, horrible way to die," Rakansaur said

"My condolences, why did they remove him" Principle asked gently

"Because of you, they believe that we are the owners of the island, your food is ours, they have been made since I discovered you on this side of the island" he told them

"Thanks for telling us," Scoutina said

"There one more thing, the new self-declared leader Grawl has vowed to ignore all the agreements we made with you over hunting rights and borders, I wrote a letter to give to Urk, I didn't want a messenger to bring it in case they are secretly supporting Grawl, I planned to leave it by your navy ship or fort, but then I bumped into you," Rakansaur said

"Ah right thanks for telling us, we will be on our guard, and you can trust me we won't tell a soul you told us this information," Scoutina said smiling

"Anyway, I better be off before Grawl and his new council notice that I disappeared," Rakansaur said as he turned

"Thank, you for the warning, Rakansaur, you have put yourself at risk to warn us of this information, thank you that's incredible," Principle said truly thankful for the courage of Rakansaur

"Have you got a light?" Said Rakansaur

"I've got a match," Scoutina said handing it to him as Rakansaur lit it and set fire to the letter that was meant to go to Urk that was meant to inform them of the events of the revolution. Scoutina and Principle left first to make sure no other colony members of both sides were watching their every footstep, fortunately, the coast was clear and Rakansaur dashed towards his border made his way back across the collapsing bluff and sat down on a wooden bench on the cliff.

Search parties were looking for him later and they found him still sitting on the bench, he had stayed there making it look like he had gone for a walk as if he knew something was up if he walked back down in daylight it would have looked suspicious, his reasoning for not being at camp was that he went for walk in the woods needing some air and had got lost and had found that bench waited for someone to find him.

The next day had dawned and Kanstunip's dead body still hung in the centre of the camp, Grawl wanted it to remain as a Message to all Kanstunip's Supporters that he was in charge now, the change that day was immediate, the new council issue laws, building farms and a prison. A new law was signed stating anyone who was not loyal could have their tents removed from them and they would have to sleep outside.

Meanwhile, Principle Chaired a meeting with All of His departments, all were Present Woody, Apple, Scoutina, Hunter, Mertyn Newly created Sheriff, and Urk, the topic would be Rakansaur's Warning of The Events of the other Colony

"Thank you, everyone, for joining me everyone, this is of the uttermost importance, Yesterday I was made aware by someone who for his safety we will keep undisclosed, warned us of a revolution that has taken place in the other colony, Where Kanstunip has been toppled and has been executed, this informant warned us of the new leader's intent to forgo the agreements made on borders, food, so I'm simply asking all of you to try to be vigilant out there so we do not provoke" Principle urged while stressing calm and the important act of not telling anyone outside of this room "If anyone finds out who told us this, they could be put in danger, words have reached my ears of the brutal death of Kanstunip," Principle said with his heart

"We need to be careful about what we do, these are troubling times, we need to not add more trouble on top, we don't need double trouble, in fact, no trouble at all would be nice, we need to maintain this business of usual sort of vibe I think," Said Mertyn

Over the following three weeks, not much happened until a messenger arrived to give a letter to the principal, which he opened and read it

Dear Principle

*"I am Grawl, I have recently taken over as the new leader of the Western Colony, and would*

*like to meet with you and discuss the elements of this trade deal negotiated between you and my predecessor Kanstunip, Tomorrow at Midday on top of the collapsing bluff"*

*Grawl, Leader of the Western Colony*

Principal re-read the letter and was conflicted and sought Urk's advice "Well, you must do what you feel is right, compromise where we must and when we can't don't" he told Principle

The principal decided that he was going to meet him and negotiate. Hunter and Scoutina were hesitant about this meeting but both trusted Principle and backed him, nonetheless.

Principle and Urk left early around ten past eleven which they knew the time from the sundial that had been found by the acting head of the scout department Ugona a few days prior. The pair had left early to get there first to give the impression that they were the superior colony, the more punctual, they were attempting a game of powerplay, they waited for ages with Grawl finally turning up over forty-five minutes late he walked over to principle "You must be principle, I'm Grawl, new leader here, I understand you had a deal over trade with Kanstunip who has resigned and has left the island" Grawl told him not knowing that they knew what had happened

"He resigned, and he left the island, how did he leave the island" Principle replied his acting was top-notch in showing genuine surprise, playing the illusion well that he had no idea at all "A few weeks ago, he woke up one morning and he said Grawl, I'm tired of this Fuck Shit and I'm tired of leading, he said here are my documents and I'm resigning you're the new leader of the Western Colony, rule it well," Grawl said thinking his version of the events was sinking in "His boat left three weeks ago the day after he resigned," said Grawl

"His Boat, he got a boat off, if we could have a look at this boat, we sort of want to get off the island, is this boat still somewhere near" said Principle who was acting quite melodramatically

"Well, for now, let's just say his life just sailed away" Grawl said laughing not noticing Principle was becoming rather nauseous and his face was going green, Urk however had noticed and stepped in and gave him a sip of water from the goblet he had brought with him to hide there hidden knowledge.

The two men sat down at a now laid table Principle was a well-mannered man, with short brown hair and stood roughly around Five foot nine and a half and had a clean shaved face, whereas the man opposite was a mammoth of a man stood around six-foot-six, and weighed around two hundred and fifty pounds and had dark shady eyes, and was quite noticeably young looking "You see these agreements Kanstunip went ahead with are far too hard on us, we simply ask the border be moved simply this way a few hundred feet" He got up "So from here to here, the new border would be here" He placed down a quick marker "You want the border to move a few hundred feet?, Okay but no more" Principle said

"Brilliant, thanking you muchly," Grawl said as the meeting ended and the border was moved. They all began to walk back to their encampment" You should not have done that" Urk insisted

"Do what?" Principle asked

"Appease him," Urk said

"We did as he asked, why look for trouble when none exists" Principle responded

"He wants a hundred today, who's to say tomorrow he doesn't come back and ask for two hundred, then four hundred, then eight hundred and then eventually they'll have the whole fucking island under his big red thumb," Urk said with concern as that were both walking back down the hill towards the camp.

The next few days were stormy with what could have been a hurricane coming through the trees cracked and split in the winds, all of the departments were told to stay indoors until it passed, this order was given because a Scout whose name was Mendoorugu was killed when the wagon he was going to get blew towards him and he got pushed against the end of the fort and fell this death off the side of the cliff, his body was located further down the cliff by the hunters, they then pushed his dead body off the overhang below, giving him a funeral at sea. For the other camp, it was far worse tents were gone, Trees were falling, and one poor sod got impaled by a spike that snapped off a tree in the high winds. Grawl though did not care in his wooden house that he had gotten others to build he was safe; he even had a fireplace in there, so he was warm and looked after while the others were out there bracing the elements. His council was changing laws and rules each day as Urk insisted that he would Grawl came back and asked for the border to be moved which Principle quite rightly said "No" but caved in when Grawl threatened to march across the border and ransack anything they had built.

At the other camp which Principle had named Mendoorugu after the scout who fell to his death off the cliffs, Tensions were rising over the food rights, and everything was going one way at the time. The days were growing colder, and the days were getting darker.

# Chapter Seven: Fuse

Hunter set up plans for a fishing trip for his Team as a way of letting off steam for their hard work, they woke up early that morning and headed off for their day off, they walked up by the fort and headed in the way of the where the mine is located and into the woods in that direction and headed down the path which led to the beach on that side, they walked down there and began to set up their fishing lines, and after around fifteen minutes they were fishing. Hunter did not go on the fishing trip himself he had elected to help Principle and Urk draft up a new constitution with new rules to help with the constant pressure from the other colony.

Meanwhile, the hunters on their fishing trip were having a whale of a time it was peaceful and really quiet, "I think I've got one, I've got a fish" a hunter shouted as his line was getting tight it was a big fish after many minutes of holding onto the fishing line until the guy finally pulled the fish out it was massive a three foot big, it was revealed to be a large pufferfish. All the others began to put their lines back into the water and the fishing commenced. They sat there for over an hour until they decided to call it a day on the fishing and decided to go and have a swim in the sea, one of the hunters swam down and saw a coral reef which the hunters quickly gave the name The Hanging Platform Reef due to its position on the side of sea ridge that drops down some thirty feet around about seven hundred and fifty yards out at sea.

the sea was quite shallow in some parts only two feet deep about a hundred yards out the beach would slope up gradually meaning the further the tide was inland the deeper the sea would be, and the shoreline at low tide would be roughly seventeen feet underwater at high tide, The cove they were in, had been found a few weeks prior and given the Name the bay of the Treacherous Abyss, given the name on how jagged and scraggy some of the cliffs were as the island turns and creates the cove.

The sea was really cold, but they had been doing really hot work earlier on so that did not seem to bother them, after an hour they got back to the beach dried off and went back to fishing which they had a lot more success this time the wagon that they brought with them was filled to the brim with pufferfish, Salmon, Cod all different varieties of fish.

On the other hand, Hunter sat in Principle's office and was in deep conversation on the new rules for the colony, they were joined by Urk, Woody and Apple, and Ugona filled in for scoutina who had yet not returned to her duties as head of scouting department. The Laws were as follows.

- Rule 1. Movements on the collapsing Bluff must be Monitored.
- Rule 2. Food and Supplies will be moved away from the Village and stored in a secure location in the event of an incursion.
- Rule 3. A marshal must be appointed.

"These rules will be implemented next week and will be enforced for however long they are necessary, Good Work everyone "Said Principle as he rose and towered over everyone at the table and walked out the room with Urk following moments later, after a few moments they all began to disperse back to whatever they were doing.

Nestled within the embrace of majestic hills, the enchanting forest beckons with its lush greenery and vibrant life. Towering trees reach towards the heavens, their branches adorned with a kaleidoscope of flowers that blanket the forest floor in a riot of colours. Animals roam freely, their presence adding to the rich diversity of this thriving ecosystem. From the graceful deer that gracefully navigate through the undergrowth to the playful squirrels that scamper along the branches, the forest is a symphony of life. The abundance of vegetation nourishes this ecosystem, creating a harmonious landscape where every plant and creature coexists in perfect harmony. Exploring this mesmerizing forest is an invitation to immerse oneself in nature's embrace and witness the awe-inspiring beauty of the natural world. They were at peace, they were at one with nature, until a noise came out of the wilderness, a fiery voice "Look what we have here, some lost birds, like some cattle rampaging across our border" a guy said with a menacing gloat.

"Actually, you are on our land the border is over two miles that way" they said pointing in the direction of where the collapsing bluff would be on the north side of the island, whereas they were on the south side of the island "Lies, This is our land, you crossed the border, to steal our food, did you not, did you not" the guy fired back

"We have not stolen anything; this is our side of the island now get lost" Bagdia of the hunting group said.

"You see" The guy fired back whilst turning to his men "Grawl was right, this Principle has plans to undermine our agreements with them for their desires, foolish, what a stupid fool" The guy turned back to the other colony's hunters.

"Those agreements were null and void weeks ago as soon as Grawl violated every single one, we violated nothing, you violated everything," Bagdia said sternly.

"Lies, you lie even now, leave our lands or face a fate worse than death" the guy boomed.

"what's your name?" Bagdia asked.

"Vyndeck, now move out of our lands this insistent face our almighty might will make you quake like the literal dogs you are, go now or else" Vyndeck shouted brandishing an axe and waving it in a threatening manner. However, the hunters stood their ground not going to budge from some brute "We will not move, we will not bow down, this is our side of the island, so you go away now or else" Bagdia said with all the other hunters standing their ground. "Someone's got some balls then, you will face it then, Group Ready Three - Two- One ATTACK" Vyndeck shouted until he was silenced by an almighty roar a huge cracking sound emerged it then eased out and peace resumed for the time being with both looked around for a quick second to see what could have made that noise. Until Vyndeck relaunched the attack as they prepared to charge a sudden disturbance shattered the peaceful ambiance. A landslide, triggered by the relentless forces of nature, sent fragments of earth cascading down the steep slopes. The cracking noise reverberated through the dense foliage, causing the ancient trees to tremble in response. The once lush and vibrant forest now bore the scars of this dramatic event, with upturned roots and displaced rocks dotting the landscape. Yet, amidst the chaos, nature's resilience shone through as delicate wildflowers bravely sprouted amidst the debris, symbolizing the unwavering spirit of life in the face of adversity, the same could not be said for Vyndeck and his men as they had been swept away with the passing Landscape and had disappeared down with a tumultuous and violent roar. "Shit the bed, we need to get back and tell hunter and principle," Bagdia said as they all grabbed their wagons of fish and walked back with the food and supplies that they had gathered from their fishing day.

They all tried to remain positive but the thoughts of what had happened to the other colony's hunters and what could potentially transpire from such events, The walk back was a silent one, filled with unease and uncertainty, once they had got back to the camp with their trophies of the hunters, they gave all the fishes to Apple, When Hunter wandered over and said "How was it?" but they did not reply "What's the Matter with all of you tonight?" Hunter said again but still with no answer nor any reply "What Happened."

"The other colony's Hunters, they threatened us, told us to back off, saying it was their land" Bagdia murmured.

"So, What Happened?" Hunter asked losing his patience.

"Landslide, as they tried to attack the north ridge slid off and crashed down, their hunters went with it," Bagdia said nervously Hunter looked at him not worried and mumbled for him to forget about it, but they still told Principle just to be on the safe side. But as far as they were concerned there was nothing, they could do about it, and nothing would result from it.

## Chapter Eight: The Missing Men

The Western Colony grew nervous there scouting team had failed to return, so much so that Grawl launched a search party, they walked across the collapsing bluff, yet found nothing, there was no sign of them in the forests, they were not at the camp, their whereabouts were just completely unknown, they had in essence completely disappeared, they looked through bushes, up trees, yet nothing. Until Dusk had turned to night and Grawl had given the order to abandon the search party, and all would return to camp, the Western Hunters would have to wait till morning to be rescued.

The next morning the hunters had still not returned, and a second scouting party was despatched to locate them, they walked up the hills to the east and moved further along to the border on the collapsing bluff. Another team looked down the cliffs towards the beach on the west coast and there was nothing there ever. Grawl was nervous, it had been at least Thirty-Six hours since they left the encampment and had not returned. His eyes were twitching, his hands shaking the thoughts going through his head were that they had defected and ran away across the border, the thought of this made his blood boil and his head shake. the fear that they had defected was squashed later the next day when a search party member came across Vyndeck wounded but alive, scattered around rubble and debris, the order was then given to get Grawl and bring him there, by the time Grawl had arrived the bodies of five members of the three-hunting team had been exhumed from the dirt of the landslide. "Vyndeck what happened," Grawl said imposingly which made Vyndeck blatantly lie "We had walked down to the ridge up there and saw the other Hunters from the eastern Colony, wheeling wagons of fish up, we told them this is our land, and that is our food, they said no, Said that Grawl was not a legitimate leader and became aggressive and marched forwards forcing us to fall back into this landslide, murdered, murdered we were," Vyndeck said lying through his teeth causing Grawl to rise to his fullest height and with a great flame of anger roared "Principle has started a war, they struck first and we will strike back ten times harder, back to camp," Grawl said as they all walked back with Vyndeck on a stretcher, with the other bodies that they had managed to locate being carried back, there were fears some of the bodies may never be found.


The Western Colony began to gather where they had done the two months prior for the execution of Kanstunip whose body had only been taken down the week before last his naked body had been left hanging for nearly two months, Grawl walked up and stood on the platform and he paused for a brief moment taking in the Applause before he began to speak "We have found our Hunters, Buried under rubble pushed towards a landslide by members of the other colony, Principle and his colonists have declared war on us with this plain violation, we burn down there village, we make them pay, Fight back, They started this war, but it will be us that strike hard and trust me we will strike hard. and they will learn you do not pick a fight with those of us who own this island" Grawl roared with great anger in a captivating speech that spark shouts "Death, Death, Death to Principle" as they chanted away. Rakansaur stood at the back and could not believe his eyes, All the work he had done all the treaties had gone up with the fires and flames of war, He knew something wasn't right if they had attacked now why did they not do it under Kanstunip something did not sit right with him, and he was determined to try and find out what it was, He went to visit Vyndeck in the hospital, and sat down to ask him a few questions, "What Happened Vyn" Rakansaur asked his former Department member who had been promoted months ago

"We had walked down to the ridge Rakansaur and saw the other Hunters from the eastern Colony, wheeling wagons of fish up, we told them this is our land, and that is our food, they said no, Said that Grawl was not our legitimate leader and became aggressive and marched forwards forcing us to fall back into this landslide, murdered, murdered we were," Vyndeck said keeping his fabricated story in sync with what he told Grawl "Okay well get well soon," Rakansaur said looking at Vyndeck's facial expression he knew something was up and he could see it in Vyndeck's face, he had told Grawl what he wanted to hear whether it was true or false.

He had a choice to make, sit back and watch Innocent people die, or risk the wrath of his colony and warn them, he opted for the latter and began to plan his route to make sure he would not be discovered, he had decided to walk towards the hills to the west then switch and go up the lesser known path and make for the collapsing bluff when there he would plan out the second phase.

The first phase went smoothly he was able to sneak away undetected and began to go towards the western hills, which lead to the western beach, upon reaching that hill he turned upwards and walked up the lesser-known path that also took you up towards the Collapsing bluff, it was a rather hot day most likely around 35 degrees Celsius quite high for later in the year, the sweltering temperature meant that Rakansaur had to take a breather but after five minutes he began to push on and make for the border and warn them off the coming disaster. The day was getting old it was about five o'clock when he reached the border and walked towards the location of the mine that he had been shown by Principle and Scoutina, upon arriving there it was night and he walked into the Mine and saw the scouts was once again Led by Scoutina "Rakansaur, what are You doing here?" said Scoutina.

"I Have to warn you, something terrible will happen," said Rakansaur with the uttermost urgency.

"What, What Is it" replied Scoutina.

"Our Hunters were killed in a landslide two days ago the one survivor, Vyndeck head of our hunters, claimed that they fell into the landslide after being attacked by your Hunting department" Rakansaur said quickly.

"I heard about this, they attacked our hunters, they brandished axes, and were quite a way on our side of the border, they moved forwards, and the landslide took them," Scoutina told them.

"I thought so, I thought that Vyndeck was telling Grawl what he wanted to hear, Grawl was enraged he's ordered an attack on your village, I needed to warn you" shouted Rakansaur.

"We need to get back there and warn them," said Scoutina about to go until she was stopped in her tracks by the sound of impounding force, they looked at the mine and saw a group of fires and pitchforks running past through the bushes, "I think it is too late," Rakansaur said.

"Right, everyone I want you to move further into the cave, Ugona take that wooden torch out and go further down the cave, Bordan put the others out we do not want to lure them here, we need to go down the caves and wait there till morning until they have withdrawn. Scoutina sat with her head against the cave wall with her hands over his crying eyes she wiped her eyes and looked towards Rakansaur who was sitting next to her "How many people will die" said Scoutina.

"Too many" Replied Rakansaur who was holding Scoutina's cold wet hand.

"Why are you helping us, Rakansaur, you didn't have to, you aren't one of us?" Said Scoutina looking into Rakansaur's eyes "Because it is the right thing to do, I found your colonists, I made mine aware of your colony's existence, I started this, I brought this upon you, I could have not told Kanstunip about your people. If I did Grawl wouldn't be attacking and Kanstunip would still be alive, all this death is because of me and me alone" Said Rakansaur with tears now streaming from his eyes "I failed, I failed Kanstunip and I failed you guys —" the sound of Scoutina's wet lips met Rakansaur's unaware dried ones until he livened up and brought himself to kiss her back they remained like this for over half a minute until she grabbed one of his small hands and wrapped it in her slightly bigger hands and began to speak "You did everything you could, without you we would not be here, without you we would not have been aware of Grawl's intentions to take as many lands as possible, if there's anyone who has failed then Rakansaur it by lord isn't you, Kanstunip would be very proud of you" said scoutina sweetly. The mood in the cave was one of fear and dread everyone they knew could be dead before the hour was out and they were powerless to do anything about it. Grawl's Soldiers quickened up their pace as they ran past the Navy ship and moved towards the old fort. The Eastern Colony lay unaware of the events that had transpired and were unprepared for the calamity that was about to hit them.

At the Colony it was a quiet night, there was entertainment a group of colonists had created their music the lyrics went like this.

*There was a time, when I was at sea, facing the island valleys from here, through the island core and island gain, we stand and rose we stand and rose across the islands core, my home came to me, my home came to thee Oohra oohra.*


*There was a time, when I was at sea, facing the island valleys from here, through the island core and islands gain, we stand and rose we stand and rose across the islands core, my home came to me, my home came to thee Oohra oohra.*

*There was a time, when I was at sea, facing the island valleys from here, through the island core and island gain, we stand and rose we stand and rose across the island core, my home came to me, my home came to thee Oohra oohra oohra oohra oooohraaaaa.*

The song that they had created was made from an ensemble of flute players, drummers and one lead vocalist, in which all the musical instruments were created by them and by hand, Hunter and his hunters were sat at the canteen eating what was left over of their evening meal. Woody and Urk were in discussion about what looked to be like a proposed new building. Overlooking the village, the Western colony emerged from the bushes there stood Grawl red and wearing black paint across his face trying to look like a traditional Celtic warrior. He towered over his colony and they gleamed back as he began to roar "Witness our might, stand united Brothers, Sisters, with me, as one for the island and for glory, Attack!" said Grawl bellowing as they made the charge towards the other village, those in the village saw a wall of fires heading towards them, 30 yards across and moving ever so fast, Hunter and Urk turned to each other and tried to form a plan of action but there was no time, they had entered the village with their torches and had begun to set the buildings on fire and hack people down. Leaving a trail of blood in their wake followed by the carnage of destruction.

For a brief period of around thirty minutes, they moved from building to building burning all in the path until Grawl gave the order to withdraw, as they had done enough for one night and they would return tomorrow to finish off their enemies, the withdrawal happened, Urk and Hunter had managed to get as many people as they could to safety. Principle who was down at the farm with Apple knew not of the events that had transpired. It was business as usual for him and Apple who were about to face a grim revelation, they had just finished going through what was in the ground when the Messager arrived "Principle" said the boy.

"Yes, what is it" asked Principle quickly.

"Emergency from Urk, Sir, Grawl's Attacked the colony, Countless dead, Colony on fire," Messenger said.

"What" said Principle and Apple at the same time.

"The colony is burning, Grawl has attacked, Appointed Colony Sherif Mertyn is dead" Pacy the messenger said.

"We need to get back there quickly, Apple come with me," said Principle as they began to run back up the path towards the village but by the time, they got back they had withdrawn all that was left was the burning buildings that were too big to be able to be put out, Principle Arrived back finding Urk and Hunter doing everything they could do to function a recovery mission to try and put out the fires and help the injured. "How Many Dead," Shouted Principle who was running over.

"Five dead, at least fifteen injured," said Urk.

"Where did they go?" asked Principle.

"They withdrew around ten minutes after we sent the message to you" replied Hunter.

"We need to try and get these fires out and prepare lookouts if anything steps across our border I want to know" ordered Principle who had taken charge of the situation. The Eastern Colony had a long night ahead of them.

Elsewhere Grawl and his men returned to their camp and sat down and ate a huge meal that their catering team had begun to create a high-carb meal of roast chicken and potatoes, carrots, runner beans and little bits of sausage and bacon.

Grawl and his leaders planned out an attack for the next day that would destroy the Eastern village. Before they prepared for a great and glorious night's sleep. the Opposite could be said for the other colony which had fallen into a haunted and restless sleep. The next day another attack came and went fortunately Scoutina and Rakansaur his only colony believed that he had died in the battle found the principal who got all the colony to go down into the mines, where the opening was completely hidden by shrubs and no lighting in the bigger parts of the caves meant it was completely dark, they hid by the hot spring which was at least a mile or more in the cave. Grawl could not understand where they had gone but he nonetheless continued the attacks on the now destroyed settlement to show his power and might but that was not proving anything as no one was there to even experience his so-called power and might so the further attacks be completely and utterly a waste of manpower.

## Chapter Nine: All Or Nothing

Deep in the mines, deep within a labyrinth of windy and twisty tunnels, the eastern colony hid within them, their disappearing act for the moment was paying off,

A meeting in the old room that was once the office of Captain Thomas Charles Henry, the island's Former Governor, "We must act and we must act now" Scoutina said.

"We must negotiate, this is a lost cause," Apple said.

Negotiate, we have tried that already Apple, look what it has led to utter chaos, are village destroyed, our people dead," Have we not learnt our Lesson? you cannot reason with a rhino, while it is trampling you to death,

"We need to attack," Woody said.

"How many of us will die too, but on the other hand negotiations could mean we lose everything" said Urk who was standing against the door, while Principle sat on an old dusty wooden chair. Scoutina, Apple and Woody sat at the other chairs with Hunter standing at the back. All went quiet with them all sharing glances until it was broken by Principle who leaned forward "Fear is not permanent, darkness does not banish out light, but light does not always trump darkness, but it's the courage to stand up against the emerging dark and fight for what's right that's what counts, if we surrender we will be pushed over if we fight we will die, so we need to fight but it needs to be on our terms" Principle said leaving all the others mesmerized about what had just gone on and the speech "we will have to come up with plans we can't be held up here for days" Apple said

"How long can we hold up here" asked Principle.

"A few weeks maybe a few months" said Hunter.

"So, we have more time than we are letting on that is slightly more reassuring," said Principle.

"Yes Slightly" Apple replied.

"We need to get more Supplies" added Scoutina.

"They don't know about the farm so the crops will be okay, my department will be fine, I will look after my team," said Apple.

"Thats good, take your department there and stay there, but if they find the farm and try and attack do not engage and get out, that's an order" Principle said firmly.

"Apple take the food we had left in storage at the colony if it's not burned that will be better so the Grawls men don't get to it and loot it for their agenda," Hunter said as he, Woody, Apple and Urk all left leaving Scoutina still sitting there Principle turned towards Scoutina "Scoutina, Scoutina," He said shaking her "Scoutina" She snapped out of it "Principle sorry, I forgot where I was then," Scoutina said

"Want to talk about it?" Principle said as he pulled a chair next to her.

"Um yes," she said.

"Well, what's on your mind?" said Principle who looked at her confused.

"Well, we got Rakansaur here" She replied.

"Yes, we got Rakansaur here?" He said raising an eyebrow.

"He could give us pages of information on their encampment, Afterall he helped build it, I mean he was Kanstunip's Second in command for

Christ's sake, so he would know their layout inside out and upside down, we could create a plan of attack from his info that would overrun them from all sides, follow them where they go, we could stop Grawl," Said Scoutina regaining her confidence and standing tall finally shaking off her trauma of the abuse she had suffered previously

"Thats a brilliant idea, go and Speak to him and get information, you will tell no one just me about this," said Principle swearing her into total secrecy as she got up out of her seat and left the room and went to find Rakansaur who was sat someone having a drink of water upon seeing him she walked over and looked down at him and he looked at her "Rakansaur can you please come with me, there's something I must discuss with you it's a matter of great importance," Said Scoutina helping him to his feet and leading him to somewhere quiet "Why are we going deep in the tunnel?" asked Rakansaur

"Because we have reason to believe we have been infiltrated, and we can't risk letting this information I'm about to give you get out" Whispered Scoutina

"Well, what is it?" Rakansaur asked.

"Me and Principle were suggesting you know lots about the other colony, well you're from it well you were principle considering inviting you to join us, but you could give us tons of information on how your colony was made and ways we could attack it from to stop Grawl?" asked Scoutina.

"Yes" Rakansaur asked.

"Well, um, would you consider in this book writing down everything you know please?" Scoutina asked with puppy dog eyes.

"Of course, I may need a few days though there's quite a lot to write and trust me I will tell no one of this" Rakansaur said kindly as he took the book and over the next few days, he began to write a huge dossier of information. By the time it was done, that book carried a great amount of detail about all the topics that they had wanted. Principle was pleased with Rakansaur as he believed it took a great deal of courage to stand against his people, but he did it anyway for the greater good his book was named Rakansaur's Diary and looked like this...

*We arrived on the island, and on some date, we knew nothing of who we our or who we were so that probably does not matter, at the start there were fights and squabbles but they sort of cut out when our leader Kanstunip was appointed leader by a vote of sticks and stones quite literally, we established a small colony on the banks of the little beach or as we called it the cove of the two horned peaks, which is accessible by the main path leading to the woods then leading on to the collapsing bluff beyond that, another path the one I used to get here, a few days ago, leads up the west hill which in turn leads to old Harry's lighthouse, a lighthouse a few hundred feet of shore but exposed on the beach at low tide, there we found an old book from a midshipman whose name was harry, who as the book says was the last man off the island as the boats were departing. The lighthouse had a lot of old tools such as axes but they weren't good for chopping trees so we built a colony of tents instead, I was leader of the Hunting department and this is where I come in on one particular morning I awoke early and had set my sights on going hunting for more food and doing some exploring I got my team together we left early and walked across what we now call the collapsing bluff until I was startled, by a girl who was slightly taller than myself, I was startled initially albeit because we had no idea there was another settlement on the island, rather than pursue violence of which I am one hundred percent against, I sent for my leader Kanstunip and they sent for there's Principle and Diplomatic talks begin my position changed in the days ahead I became ambassador for diplomatic relations as well as Deputy leader of the colony, it became my job to oversee diplomatic relations, which I succeeded in getting the trade deal over the line but the crisis was coming and there was no avoiding it, we tried everything and anything to resolve it but at last nothing worked the tent colony we had built which was very good from what we had available until the storms came and came, people died from hyperthermia, being blown away. A member of the crafting department Grawl became furious by the problems believing that Kanstunip the short man was sucking up to the eastern colony to get supplies and not doing what was the rightful thing to do and just go and take it as in his eyes it was not yours, to begin with, and all deaths of our colony men were on him. There had been unease in the air for a great many says the sheer amount of meetings we had was off the chart, but as it seemed at the time I seemed to be the only one who wanted to try and do anything about it and one fateful day it happened the Coup the people became frustrated and had had enough of Kanstunip to the point they stripped his clothes to his naked body and dragged his body through mud like he was some sort of animal, it became worse Grawl taking over and executing Kanstunip then picking up his body and tying him to the hanging rope for two months until he was a skeleton floating around with the wind. All those in the cabinet executed me trying everything I could is the only thing I can think of that saved my life. I had no part in the Grawl cabinet and quite frankly I wanted no part of it either. On the day of the Hunting team's demise, I was replaced as ambassador by some random person even though the position was non-existent after Kanstunip's death, with regards to the placement there are three potential points of attack*

- *path One: To the Collapsing Bluff*
- *Path Two: up the western hill and the eastern path towards the forest at the top*
- *Path Three: between both paths, there is a hidden one that goes towards the bay that leads to your cove where your hunters came across ours*

*To attack from this one would need to have one pinned down why one probe another here I would say it's highly unlikely an attack at just one would do anything to your, well our now numerical disadvantaged but what I would further state is that your technology is far more advanced to anything that they have, but as they say Numbers's don't necessarily win the battle but they help a great deal, so to win against them a great offensive and defensive strategy will probably need to be used. another path you can is, but is a little overgrown there's a cliff on the inside with thick vines that skilled people could abseil down but, I stress that that is probably the most unsafe route but again quite a logical move as there would be no guards on that side at all as why have guards looking over at a cliff as no one's stupid enough to attempt it, but it would make a good distraction, that could help in the long-run as they look towards the cliffs that's when you make your move, it's like a game of chess first you manoeuvre your marks into position then you attack, I believe for you to be successful all of the aforementioned things need to be in order then and only then can we be successful In this mission to stop Grawl, Grawl I will speak in more detail about.*

*Grawl is a very manipulative individual who believes has an enormously powerful aurora that he parades around with if you ask me though it's a posh world for toilet seat, all jokes side he is a very strong individual capable of carrying well over two to three hundred pounds of weight and his physical size is well on his side he must stand at the moment somewhere In the six foot five six foot six region if more, but as they say, the bigger they are the harder they fall,*

*I cannot describe his key allies as, to be perfectly honest, I do not know enough about them to even go into any detail at all, I am afraid, but I hope this information is enough for you to be able to plan with. Signed – Rakansaur*

The amount of information that he had written and given to them was impressive he had given them at least 4 and a half pages of information of the highest order which meant Scoutina could now go back to Principle with these key details, and he would then decide if this plan was to you know go ahead. "Well, Scoutina I have read it, and this seems like an idea that's coming to fruition, but there are still a through gaps we need to discuss, but for now be reassured I have read the document in its entirety and the positives outweigh the negatives, get these sorted and come and see me again," said Principle.

"Okay, Principle" replied Scoutina.

"Oh wait, one moment, I've decided Rakansaur's got a place amongst us, he has been a great friend of us he is one of us" Principle said smiling.

"Okay, I'll go tell him" Scoutina said as she turned.

"You like him, don't you?" said Principle looking at her as if he knew something.

"Well I mean, he's a really lovely person and a handsome individual, so yes why wouldn't I?" Scoutina said blushing.

"I'm happy for you, he's an honourable man to reveal key secrets and details about his former colony and his former friends to save innocent people he hardly knows that takes a great deal," said Principle approvingly as Scoutina left the room closing the door behind her.

Grawl sat in his chair at his encampment, eating his tea and ready to announce another attack on the eastern colony but the question of where they were still was very much unanswered, it had been seventeen days since they had attacked the colony and sixteen since they disappeared. he sent a small party of twenty men to go and launch another attack. The men began their trek to the now burnt-down eastern colony. the walk took them around about an hour, they had changed tactics from running there and blitzing them but going slowly and catching the enemy by complete surprise. But when they got to the colony there was nothing there not wanting to waste the night decided to go and walk down the path leading to the eastern beach and see what was down there, down the hill they found what seemed to be an old settlement "I would say this must have been there first Settlement" The leader said.

"How would you guess that sir?" someone said.

"Well, the wood looks rotten, looks like it wasn't used for long and why live in his when you have that further up the hill," the man said again as they walked on towards the beach, which they discovered was massive and was dry, as the high tide does not reach this part of the beach itself. They had an idea to walk up the hill they could see at nearly the other side of the beach, they were walking across the beach there fire torches in their hands, on top of the hill which was in near complete darkness, a guy was sat down looking towards the beach he had no doubt noticed the little fires that were heading that way, upon seeing them he sprang to action and began to run back down the other side of the hill, The guy was

At the farm Apple sat in her chair having something to eat and having a drink, a few others were standing around talking about a few different topics, until the door flung open and Barn one of the farmers ran in "Grawl's men coming this way" He shouted.

"Which way?" said Apple surprisingly calm which shocked her farmers.

Down the hill towards the beach," said Barn.

"How many, how many people, HOW MANY?" Apple said quickly.

"I could only see the light of their torches, but from the sheer number of torches I'd say two dozen or more," he said nerved.

"So where isolated," Another said with everyone nervous bar Apple who stood up and looked at everyone and said with a reassuring voice "If they come here, we fight, they don't know this farm as we do, we have the home-field advantage they have to see us to attack, plus we have that gunpowder that Scoutina asked us to keep safe, it's obvious we lure them here as soon as they enter he we light it and run like hell" Apple said forming a plan. The attacking force was walking down the hill and noticed the light "Sir, there's a light" someone said.

"Your Right, so they hid further down the hill, for the glory of our camp, prepare to attack, move slowly so they don't expect us," Hortun one of Grawls appointed war leaders said as they began to crawl towards the farm, as they went through the fields, they realized that it was a farm as they could see that they had planted a huge amount of seeds and were growing lots and lots of food a fact that annoyed them as they had hardly any food at home. They continued to crawl through the large bushes to remain undetected, moving ever so slowly they were now using guerilla warfare tactics to try and get behind enemy lines. They split into key attacking forms ready to attack from a few areas to overwhelm them. they were still nowhere near the farmhouse and had gone through a cow field to get to where they needed to be, they emerged out of the darkness and used their torches as a signal method with the signal being ATTACK, they ran and burst through the farm door,

"Surrender in the name of Grawl, Oh" Hortun shouted until he realized the stone house was empty and there was nothing there they and they all breathed a sigh of relief. "I thought there was going to be something waiting for us, What a shame," Hortun said dropping his torch to the floor unbeknownst to them, Apple and her team had left twenty minutes earlier with everything of any value leaving dust on the floor giving the illusion it hadn't been used for a while but it had been reality gunpowder and the torch dropping engulfed Grawls men in one great **BOOM,** a huge fireball went up in the sky, the blast could be heard for miles around Principle and Scoutina heard the blast from the opening of the mine "What on Earth was that," Principle said whilst turning to Scoutina. Meanwhile, at the other end of the island, Grawl heard the blast and looked towards his lieutenants "What do you think that was" He asked.

"No idea sir, but if you don't mind, I'm going to retire to bed" The guy said.

"Ok, Nighty Night, Hurgentile" said Grawl showing what looked to be a little compassion.

Back at the farm, the Farmhouse was still standing, it had all its windows and doors blown off, and the room had disappeared and all but disintegrated as the fireball rose. everyone who had entered the building had died bar one of

Grawl's men who had been thrown through a window in the explosion, he rolled around as he was on fire and lost one of his eyes from the initial explosion. The farmers returned to inspect their work, the man saw them brandished his axe and was prepared to fight h went forward for Apple and the people behind them but was stopped in his tracks by someone who snook up behind him and struck him knocking him out and saving his fellow farmers. the decision to take the guy's body and drop him at the collapsing bluff was made, they left him there and returned to the mine. "Apple, we heard a huge noise last night you would have been further down the hill in that direction do you have an idea what could have caused it" asked Principle.

"I do, it was, we saw Grawl men coming towards the farm, and we had no way to get out, so we used that gunpowder that we found at the fort, and we coated the floor in it, then secretly left out the backdoor, they burst in  One of his lieutenants dropped his torch to the floor as breathing a sigh of relief we weren't there but it set off the gunpowder killing them all, we took out the one survivor and dumped his body on their side of the collapsing bluff" Apple informed Principle

"Good, Good, you used your initiative and kept your team alive I'm so proud of you, great work" he said hugging her, there was some resolve that night something positive finally happened.

Grawl's men later that day found the survivor and he was brought back immediately to their encampment where he was interrogated for what had happened, "We found their farm, it had light glowing from it so we attacked it, it was empty, Hortun dropped his torch in relief that it was empty and it emerged what we fought was dust on the floor was Gunpowder, that ignited with the dropping torch, there dead, they're all dead now" He said

"How did you survive then?" Grawl said menacingly.

"The explosion threw me through the outside window, all the others were thrown against the walls as the fireball went up through the roof and into the sky," he said back.

"How did you end up at the Collapsing bluff," Grawl said.

"I can't say, sir, I can't remember anything after being thrown through the window" the guy said not remembering about being knocked out by members of the other colony. Grawl looked down on the man confused by his story but not confused enough to want it to be investigated.

Scoutina and Rakansaur sat at a desk discussing some extra details on the other colony "on the matter of layout how is it structured" asked Scoutina jotting down notes on a spare bit of paper "Well towards the Hill is the sleeping quarters, they are probably around eight feet long and are about five feet from each other there are small paths laid between them, each tent has a bed and seat, quite primitive really but it did its purpose, the eating quarters is next across the street which the long roads runs down the separating the tent area from the food area, the food area's a wooden hut that was built and you sit down on some tree stumps around there that have been made into chairs, the pleasure area, was a large green area which was great for walking and just sitting and relaxing in general, the next and last area is the storage area which is right at the back and is where we would keep a lot of our storage" Rakansaur answered the question giving key information that could be used for the plans "Thank you for this I know it must be hard to have us asking these questions" said Scoutina kindly

"It's fine, I'm more than happy to save Innocent lies, Grawl needs to be stopped, he doesn't know that Vyndeck made up the story about the attack, but the problem is that he won't listen, so he needs to find out in some other way," Rakansaur said kindly as he stood up and prepared to leave the room and find something to eat. But stopped in his tracks and turned and said, "If anything Vyndeck should be held for account as it's his lies that brought us to this point, rather than admit that he made a mistake he opted to create a story that appeased Grawl's narrative."

"Well, first we need to find a way to get to that point, but I'm sure that will be one of the first things on the agenda when we do," said Scoutina whilst she was just finishing writing down her notes she could give them to Principle later on, which after his eyes had scanned them, the Council could later have their discussion on them later on.

Principle and Scoutina met at lunchtime to talk over the notes, at which he approved the idea, and the discussion could go ahead and was scheduled to be on the top of the agenda at the council meeting which was scheduled to begin in around two and half hours.

The meeting started dead on time with Apple. Hunter, Woody, Urk and Scoutina were all in attendance they were using the old office that they were using previously, and it remained quiet for a few moments until Principle opened the meeting "Good afternoon, Everyone, sorry for the timing of the meeting, but our lovely Scoutina, has a plan she would like to put forward, without further ado Scoutina take over" said Principle encouragingly.

"Thanks, Principle" She said standing up "I have an idea for an offensive against the other colony,

I have spoken to Rakansaur, and he has given me these notes that I have in my hand, that tell us all the routes into their encampment and all the routes that are not used. that we can attack from overwhelming them at all sides, we have an opportunity to take the fight to them and stop Grawl and make sure it is fucking permanent" Scoutina said pitching the idea with a strong tone

"It's an idea, but this could cost us everything, how many could die?" Apple said voicing a doubt.

"If we don't, we will fall, we can't hide in a cave forever, it's all or nothing for us, fight or die, we will run out of food before long or we do this," Scoutina said defending her position on the matter.

"I think this is possible but needs to be planned out to near perfection to stand a chance of pulling this off but as they say will all die one day so why the fuck not," said Hunter voicing his support on the matter.

"Urk, what are your thoughts on the matter?" Principle asked him as he was silent at the back of the room "I believe what I see I have doubts on some aspects, but on the plans themselves, we will run out of food, we cannot use this hiding charade forever, if we try to hide for much longer, they will either find us or there find us and if they find us, we will have no escape that's the one way in and the only one way out, so with this taken into account, I agree with scoutina, we must fight back and strike them before they strike us" said urk logically

"Okay, thanks Urk, We need this voted on First, I will not vote on it myself I will leave this up to the council I will have no say on the matter" Principle said he would support any outcome they opted for so they all left to vote and when they returned the ballots were placed on the table and Principle read them out "the no's to left one and the Yes's to the right three, we move to fight the other colony, Scoutina go and inform Rakansaur I want you to get him to help you plan this mission" Principle ordered

"Okay, Principle I will take the next few days to plan this out and will have the plans within the next three to four days" Scoutina said as she left the room, she walked down the small and narrow walkways and headed to find wherever Rakansaur was, it took her around half an hour to find him, "Rakansaur" she said walking over.

"Yes Scoutina, what do you need?" He asked standing up.

"I require a service of you, I have been tasked with planning the attack on the western colony, I want you to help me plan it as you know the ins and outs of their whole setup you can help us do it in a way that will avoid numerous needless casualties, please will you help me?" asked Scoutina.

"Of course, I will," said Rakansaur kindly "When do we start."

## Chapter Ten: What we must and what we can

The day started like any other, people awoke but this time they had woke earlier than usual, it was the day of the attack on the western colony, people were being moved into position, and the plan that had been drawn up by Scoutina and Rakansaur consisted of 6 different regiments one abseiling down the side of the cliffs, another going through the woods between the eastern and western path, one through the eastern path and the other three were going to go head on and draw the colony straight out so they could get the other two behind enemy lines and loop around at both edges. Rakansaur and Principle were not there, they had remained at the cave as their presence could have caused quite a few things, they would have surely killed Principle on the spot, Rakansaur though would have suffered a fate worse than death, Grawl would have used his height and weight advantage to out muscle the five foot four Rakansaur and beaten him to the pulp for not returning, and then would of Kanstunip style executed him for betraying the colony and for aiding and abetting the enemy by tapping into his vast knowledge of them and their way of life. Scoutina was leading one Regiment on one side, Woody was leading the one from the Cliffs which left the ground teams led by Hunter, Urk and Apple.

People were being put in position, as the sky was becoming brighter and much clearer, they did not have much time if it got lighter, they would see them, and it would mean the devised plans would surely fail. the three regiments were all with ten men so all together thirty men were walking towards their encampment the other thirty were waiting for the fighting to commence so they could play their part. "When do we attack sir" someone said from the back.

"We wait till the fighting begins, we are the spear, and they are the stick," Woody said as the magnitude of the task ahead began to set in, The order was given and the sound of a flute making what looked to be a war cry, erupted into the air, the noises of trotting feet and the trampling of fields went through the air, Grawl looked across and saw a sea people armed running towards them across the field "Enemy at the gates" he roared louder than ever, the sound of people scrambling as they entered through the village mowing people down, The toll on both nature and humanity was heavy, the field was littered with blood. It would take years before this field before it recovered to its formal splendour. It had become clear metal, bodies and blood had taken the place of plants, shrubs, and bushes. The fight continued and was brutal for both sides, the sound of swinging axes, the clattering of swords and the shouting of the fighters.

Back at the mine, Principle and Rakansaur sat at the office table in total silence, the room was cold and hardly lit with a single torch lighting the room, they both exchanged glances before Principle began to speak "I think the fighting will has started by now, I just pray to god we made the right decision" Principle said rubbing his left eyebrow "I just hope that when the day is out that we have survived, My heart is hurting Rakansaur, I don't think I can take the loss"

"It was always destiny that the fight should begin really," said Rakansaur.

"How can destiny, be part of my decision," Principle said confused.

the destiny that awaits will always be formed by every decision you make and in these moments of the decision you fully shape the destiny that lies right in front of you, and all you need is to be the person that you aspire to be, and the rest will follow suit" said Rakansaur stoically.

"But it's my decision, I'm scared that I'm struggling to work out if I made the right one," Principle said nervously.

"Well, I think we did personally;" Rakansaur said looking at Principle.

"Why, do you think that?" said principle.

"Well, I believe what I see, and I know the only thing that allows darkness is the lack of the light to challenge it, in time we will know whether we made the right decision, but what matters right now is we prevent further loss of life and make sure we Rideout the storm," said Rakansaur.

"Spoken, very diplomatically and very philosophically Rakansaur" principle said kindly.

Back on the frontlines, the attack was stagnating, "Withdrawal" Urk shouted as they pulled out of the village and returned to the mine. "How did it go?" Principle

"Well, it worked okay, stagnated towards the end, but they started getting the other hand, so we withdrew," said Urk slowly.

"Oh, good god," the principle said shocked.

Meanwhile, Grawl paced his tent, "We have been attacked, we must find out where they are and kill them all, get started" He shouted but someone ran in with some important information

"Sir," the guy said "We found this dust type stuff over, the storage area" before he could finish a huge fireball went up in the storage area, killing everyone who was in the area. The attack was a rouse while Woody's team abseiled in and out with the mission of sabotaging the enemy lines. Grawl ran out of his tent and immediately went to explore the damage and to see if there were survivors like everyone else did. The fireball was massive and went as far as you could see into the sky and spread to people's tents and other parts of the encampment. the outcome was bleak with lots of their supplies going up in the explosion. The inferno was raging on and the explosion and the subsequent second explosion had killed almost thirty people. Grawl went into a rage and ordered everyone to attack the colony, unbeknownst to them was that was what the other colony wanted to happen, they wanted them to follow them.

The Next day dawned and Grawl's war party prepared to move out and cross the collapsing bluff all fifty of their surviving colonists joined in on the attack, the plans were simple to scout out the other colony's hideouts and follow where they go and kill them. They set off for their final mission with everyone one hundred per cent behind the plans to attack the eastern colony. the war party moved slowly amongst the trees, being as quiet as possible the tactic they were trying to use here was one of guerrilla warfare.

The collapsing bluff was in sight and they stepped across the border someone fell onto a hidden line string which set a tripwire off that brought spikes up from under the ground, impaling a few men, those who were further back who were not affected by the first wave of the traps began to push forwards and they gradually moved more towards the fort, which they located footsteps leading down into so the order was given for half of the people present to attack them in the fort. Grawl appointed his lieutenant Handgorth to lead the attack.

The attackers charged into the Fort and searched everywhere and anywhere for the colony they stood in the main courtyard saw a sign that was written in the wall that said ***Got you- Love the Eastern Colony***, seconds after there had read that a flamed arrow went through the window from the direction of the navy ship, which they thought nothing off but suddenly realised what was happening the floor was completely covered in gunpowder "Run" Handgorth shouted but it was too late the arrow had fallen off the wall causing the floor to ignite the southside wall of the fort which was made out of hardened stone exploded sending pillows of smoke and debris down on Grawl and the others that were waiting nearby, the view from there was shocking they had seen a huge fireball erupt from the fort before the side of the wall exploded with it, half of the attacking force that was left perished in the explosion, Grawl turned to see the Eastern colony emerging from the trees, he turned to fight and went to ask his men to fight back "Prepare to attack" Grawl shouted

"No," they said.

"What is the meaning of this?" Grawl shouted.

"We won't attack look what just happened we have just been decimated; I don't know about you, but I would rather seek peace than lose my life just like those men just did" a guy said.

"Oakmill, you are naïve," Grawl said "Attack, Attack NOW, Attack Now Goddamn it" he shouted becoming increasingly angry.

"No, we will not fight no more, Oakmill said "Let's go, everyone." He said again as some people turned to leave

"No, you will go nowhere, I am the leader of this colony, I am the leader of you, and you will do what I say, and you will obey me" Grawl roared rising to his full height and trying to tower over Oakmill as high as he could get.

"You were our leader, you killed Kanstunip over him leading us badly when now you've gone cost us more lives than Kanstunip ever did, you aren't the leader anymore Grawl face the music, we will not attack, we will not follow you anymore" Oakmill said looking up at Grawl challenging his might and standing his ground.

"Whose leader now than you," Grawl said mocking him for being small and insignificant.

"Maybe," Oakmill said.

"Really," he said grabbing his arm in a tight hold and dragging him before he lifted him in the air while Oakmill was left struggling to wiggle to get free Grawls hold was too tight, so he lifted him with the other and threw him over the cliff, "Now that's done with Attack that's an order," Grawl said cockily, but they still did not move they had turned on him but before anyone can react Grawl was knocked unconscious and tied up

The Eastern colony walked over and the tied-up Grawl was handed to them, and the battle and the hostilities were over, peace had resumed, Principle was overjoyed, and the Western colony was dissolved the surviving colony members were incorporated into the Eastern colony that had now been renamed to the United Island colony of the Archipelago,

Grawl awoke in a purpose-built cell a few hours later, with Rakansaur standing outside of it "Rakansaur, you live, but you hide and don't fight, and reemerge when the fight is over the Great coward" Grawl said mockingly.

"The great coward, nice name, but you don't realise it do you, I fought more than anyone, I warned the eastern colony of your election hours after the death of Kanstunip, I warned them because I knew you would forgo agreements made, I warned them of your attack, and I planned your historic downfall, I fought more than you would possibly know, oh you don't know do you Vyndeck confessed to me a few hours ago that he fabricated the attack of the eastern colony to appease you, so you attacked innocent people on false information," Rakansaur said

"You helped destroy me, you helped bring down what you helped create" Grawl said shouting with an enthusiastic sense of anger as his eyes let off a red glow and out his ears came steam.

"I helped us create a civilisation of people that washed up on the beach, not start a war, that should never have happened in the first place, I helped destroy you not the colony, the colony is not rotten to the core, but you more or less," Rakansaur said.

"But you still helped them to destroy me nonetheless, which makes you completely culpable in this whole fiasco we now find ourselves him, you betrayed the colony, you betrayed me, what did you tell them about us, what information did you give them?" Grawl yelled in utter shock at what he had been hearing.

"I gave the Eastern colony information on our layout, I did this to save the people I care about, I protected the innocent people who did know wrong that's what any true leader would do" Rakansaur said looking down at Grawl "And the Wrath of the gods is waiting for you".

"Are they, Rakansaur, are they there really waiting for me, wow you were always a fantasist, head in the clouds I know people like you, I know your kind, the cowardice shines off you like a torch in a cave, like the moon on the ocean, and your cowardly blood will trickle down eventually as a warning to all that come in your wake, I see you Rakansaur, I SEE YOU, YOU WILL FACE YOUR JUDGEMENT SOON RAKANSAUR AND YOU WILL OBEY ME YOU WILL BOW DOWN BEFORE ME, DO YOU HERE ME!" Grawl yelled in a stream of rage but it was to no avail as the sound of the closing door emerged as Rakansaur walked out of the room. he walked up into the office and took a seat next to Principle, who was in attendance along with him was Urk, Woody, Hunter, Apple and Scoutina it was silent until Principle formally opened the meeting "Good Afternoon, thanks for coming everyone and also double thanks for coming Rakansaur, right well let's get down to the main purpose, we need a vote of what to do with Grawl, Any Suggestions" said principle as he looked around at everyone "I have one, I spoke with him earlier and he has no remorse whatsoever so I put forward execution, wait not just Execution Kanstunip style, strip him of his cloths and hang him naked, and leave his body hanging for two months" Rakansaur said laughing "I agree Principle, he killed so many people, he deserves it" Scoutina said the outcome meant that vote was to execute him at dawn but he didn't take lightly to that "EXECUTE ME, YOU CAN'T DO THAT, YOU HAVE NO RIGHT, WHO DO YOU THINK YOU ARE, YOU CAN NOT DO THIS ME, WHO DO YOU THINK YOU ARE RAKANSAUR A LITTLE RAT THAT SHOULD HAVE HAD HIS BLOODY HEAD PUT BACK STRAIGHT, A DIRTY DOG THAT SHOULD HAVE BEEN PUT DOWN BEFORE IT SPREAD IT'S VILE FLEAS. A TOAD WITH NO HOUSE IS STILL A TOAT NONETHELESS, YOU WILL NOT EXECUTE ME YOU HEAR THAT, YOU WILL OBEY ME AT ONCE I AM GRAWL COLONY LEADER, THE RIGHTFUL ISLAND LEADER AND YOU WILL OBEY ME AT ONCE" Grawl yelled in utter rage before Rakansaur looked at him "Shut up, you're not leader Kanstunip is, And no one in hell would obey you not even dog and that's pure and simple, you are being executed so sit there, keep your great pie muncher shut as you are not getting out of this one, I said the gods will condone there will" Rakansaur said putting the childish Grawl in his place

The following morning the stage had been set, and the execution was about to start Grawl was led through the colony naked and was taken to the podium that had been built within the hours, he had the rope placed around his next but was allowed to say his final words "We will allow you to say your final words" Principle said sitting in the chair at the back "such as this and such is life, I did what I did because I did it, and that's the truth of the matter, I will die not as man, but as an animal that, was ill-treated and ill-informed" Grawl said then the makeshift chair he was standing on was kicked from underneath him as his body dropped and the rope tightened until he was almost gasping from the air and squirming from side to side as he tried desperately to free himself but he couldn't as he gave his last breath and the moments later was one of shock as his naked lifeless body blew around with the wind as Kanstunip's had done months earlier.

The rest of the day they were in mourning, but they didn't exactly know why, they did not want to have to do it but felt over time that it was the right thing to do when the moment itself came, Vyndeck was also Executed for his part in the lies that had brought so much devastation and destruction to the island, although his execution was not as severe as Grawls.

The next days were the start of great advancement, Woody created plans to rebuild the colony this time the whole island was to be part of it, Principle was given the position of Lord Protector of the Island colony as they headed into a brighter more peaceful age that would hopefully progress.

The next days were hard and long, Principal permitted Woody to initiate an operation: Reset which was planned to rebuild the colony to its former glory, While Principle and Urk reviewed the original colony constitution which they planned to take out certain things as they were no longer necessary. The Document now read...

- *Rule One: Stealing is Prohibited and will carry harsh punishments.*
- *Rule Two: Over-consuming food is prohibited.*
- *Rule Three: Protect the water supply at all costs.*
- *Rule Four: There will be no discrimination of any kind whatsoever.*
- *Rule Five: there will be no running away from your appointed department.*
- *Rule Six: Hostilities will not be tolerated.*

*Signed URK – Deputy Leader of The Island Colony*

Although bleak the newly adapted constitution put in place covered most things that it needed to as the new age sailed into the brighter future the Island was at peace, and everything was back to normal well a new normal.

## Chapter Eleven: Shocks and Horrors

There was a man, quite a large man well tall but not large quite slim in a way, he was sitting In his office writing down some important documents while a big TV was blaring on the wall, he was watching Premier League football on it, the office itself was large he had a high power job, the room itself was decorated with the most up to date furniture imaginable, with armchairs laced with expensive fabric and a huge coffee table in front of the desk around the armchairs, the desk itself was made out of hard oak, this man was very wealthy and had a great deal of power. The room was lit by the sun, and it was dusk by the golden sunlight going through the windows and onto the office floor. It was quiet to quiet the only sound to be heard was the screeching of the pen hitting the paper. Then suddenly the door burst open and in walked this young girl roughly around twenty years old and tallish around five foot nine and she waltzed in smiling "We've won the Bafta" The girl exclaimed causing the man at his desk to look up "We've just won the Bafta for best drama" she said again.

"What" Shouted the man.
"Archipelago just won the bafta, for best Drama, it was announced five minutes ago," The girl said screaming.

Ruddy Fantastic," The man said lurching out of his chair and punching the air.

"What are you going to Celebrate with Sir?" said the girl.

"How about a big bottle of none of your fucking business girl, if only they knew it was real though," said the man laughing causing the girl to question "What's real, sir?" she said.

"If only they knew the truth if only, they knew why it was so real because it was real, you think the actors would go to an island to shoot this, or if they would make it look so real, because child, it is real, the truth of the story is it wasn't a story," The producer said.

"So, the death of Kanstunip and Grawl brutal TV executions have happened, that's so disgusting, and the whole world thinks it was good drama" said the girl who was about to vomit on the office floor.

"Yes, the deaths were real, which is what made the whole feel so bloody realistic," The producer said.

"So, you produced it by---" She was quickly cut off.

"Yes, I produced it, by means that are more or less illegal" The producer said.

"Why, why do it like this?" said the girl.

"Because actors, would not sign for my project, they wouldn't work for me, I needed this made, it had to be made, if you ever had the dream of a story that must be told, that must be shown, well my dear this is it, the greatest story that you will ever tell, that the world will ever see, My dream came true and I got a bloody Bafta for it too" The producer said looking down at her and laughing in a menacing but subtle way which more or less made the girl feel sort of uneasy and a little scared.

"You are bloody proud of this aren't you?" said the girl.

"Yes, Margaret I am actually, of course I am proud my show is one of the most popular of twenty twenty-three it raked in tens of millions of viewers each week from all around the globe, why wouldn't I be happy eh? Wait! you are going to report this aren't you?" exasperated the producer whose almighty smile had been taken off his smug face.

"I think I have no choice from a moral standpoint you've broken numerous laws and regulations, there's no way this can't be reported I'm afraid," said Margaret as she scanned the room and a stack of paperwork took her fancy she moved towards them and moved the top piece of paper that said in big red letters NEVER TO BE SHOWN TO PUBLIC this bold statement made her believe that there was something there that there shouldn't have been

"Not to be shown In Public," said Margaret with a cheeky glare "Looks like we got something here then, I hope there's nothing here that there shouldn't be, but looking at these red bold letters I'm guessing not probably," she said lifting the page and there was a list a gigantic list of names and lots of key documents that were located on top of them.

| Name | Age | Height | Weight | Located From |
|---|---|---|---|---|
| Principle | 21 | 5ft9 ½ | 175 pounds | Drugged at Party |
| Hunter | 22 | 6ft 3 | 220 pounds | Clinic |
| Scoutina | 18 | 5ft 7 | 198 pounds | Drugged at Party |

| Bordan | 23 | 6ft 4 | 180 pounds | Clinic |
| --- | --- | --- | --- | --- |
| Ugona | 18 | 5ft2 | 110 pounds | Drugged at party |
| Apple | 20 | 5ft 5 | 130 pounds | Drugged at party |
| Woody | 19 | 5ft 11 | 190 pounds | roadside |
| Urk | 22 | 6ft | 189 pounds | roadside |
| Hinp | 24 | 5f5 6 | 165 pounds | clinic |
| Hornup | 18 | 6ft3 | 216 pounds | Clinic |
| Nurk | 19 | 5ft5 | 101 pounds | roadside |
| Kanstunip | 24 | 5ft | 100 pounds | roadside |
| Rakansaur | 18 | 5ft 4 | 150 pounds | Drugged at party |
| Grawl | 19 | 6ft6 | 250 pounds | Football game |
| Amm | 18 | 4ft8 | 100 pounds | party |
| Vyndeck | 19 | 5ft11 | 178 pounds | roadside |

There were stacks of these documents with the names of the people who were on the island and how and where they were taken from this shocking revelation caused Margaret to take a step back as she gasped in total "What the literal fuck, they were all abducted, what was the point of listing these people, what was there purpose, what benefit do they bring" Margaret said confused as she scooped all of them up

"The benefit, the benefit of them was that they were the perfect livestock, the perfect people for the perfect story, the perfect people, not well known enough for people to care about, their disappearance means nothing necessarily, the greatest story was told, I got what I wanted and I don't care about what it took us to get it, we won we persevered, well season two here we come," The producer said laughing as he walked towards her as she stepped back and said, "So your first thought is to cash in and make season two, even though and over what has happened, the deaths of people, You utter monster, what about their loved ones?" said Margaret

"What about them, people care about the story, not about the people in the story, they are insignificant, who cares about them, I certainly don't, and neither should you, oh so sad eyes, it's not as bad as it seems, my dear," said the producer. Margaret kept getting further back as he got closer, "Not as bad, this is worse than bad, it's inhumane, it's vile on so many levels" said Margaret who was becoming visually shaken by the revelation.

"There are two types of people in the world, the useless and the useful, they were useless, and I made them useful, to them I'm a god, I gave them life," said the producer sternly "Now, girl, put these documents down now," He hissed like a snake but Margaret defiantly was still backing off still clutching the documents with both hands "Think carefully girl, don't do something you'll end up regretting," he said coldly.

"What will I regret?" Margaret said as she turned sharply and bolted for the door grabbed the handle and left the room with the documents, "MARGARET" he yelled until he went quiet and murmured "Great, I'm now in for a great Boul of shit" The producer said, "If those documents get out, then I'm going to have more bullshit against me than a farmer in a fucking cow pen, oh great **Fucking god**".

Printed in Great Britain
by Amazon